# POLL DANCER

### Push and Pole Book 1

## LAURA HEFFERNAN

*To Kerry,*

*one of the strongest people I've ever known*

# Chapter One

**Gold Rush:** This is one of my favorite moves, although for the longest time, I thought it was called "the Face Plant." With a name like that, it looks pretty much as you'd expect…

*- Push and Pole Fitness Tutorials, Vol. 2*

Hair braided neatly out of my face? Yup. Sports bra holding my girls in place? Got it. Hairspray to keep my booty shorts from riding up? Always.

After re-applying my lipstick a second time and double-checking the view from my phone's video camera, I was ready. Although I'd done half a dozen of these videos over the past few months to promote my new pole fitness classes at the local dance studio, I still got nervous every time. But social media brought in business. The only way to get over the nerves was to do the thing, so I wiped my palms against my shorts, adjusted my top one more time, and took a deep breath.

Finally, I hit "record" and moved into position. "Hey,

everyone, I'm Mel from *Push and Pole Fitness*. I'm going to do one of my favorite short routines to give you a hint of what we do. If you like what you see, come on down to my studio on Central Ave. We've got classes five nights a week. The number's in my bio. And don't forget to follow me for more videos. I put out new tutorials each week, so you can practice at home between classes."

Gripping the cold metal bar with one hand, I walked in a circle, then spun around, flashing a smile at the camera. "Don't worry. This isn't first class stuff. Just a taste of what you can achieve one day if you put your mind to it."

After a word to my phone, music blared from the Bluetooth speakers in the corners.

Every dancer has favorite songs for different moods. When I did exhibitions or contests, I preferred something with fast and slow sections to show off a variety of talents. But live streams were short, quick. The purpose was to wow the audience, show my best moves.

To blow off steam, nothing beat Whitney Houston circa 1987. Even though she was before my time, my mom used to listen to her when she'd work out. Wherever we lived, the two of us would dance together, making each new place feel like home. Whitney's songs brought me fond memories—and gave me a much-needed jolt of enthusiasm. Blasting "I Wanna Dance with Somebody," I started my routine.

Step, step, dip, twirl, down, up. Spin, climb, twirl, flip. Down to the floor, ending in a split. After the second chorus, I climbed, scooting my way to the top before clamping my legs around the pole, wrapping my torso around to the front, and balancing in a seated position. I paused for dramatic effect, looking directly at the camera.

My legs parted, and I dropped.

The ground shrieked toward me. Seconds from the bottom,

my legs snapped together, my hands tightened their grip, and I halted.

At least, that was how it was supposed to work. How it did work, the last two hundred times I exhibited the move.

Not today, though.

I fell, as planned. Then the front door of my condo flew open. The condo where I lived alone, where the door had been locked thirty seconds ago. No one else should have a key.

My head snapped involuntarily toward the sound. Time froze. My ex-boyfriend Gary stumbled across the threshold. I couldn't for the life of me think what he was doing in my home. He never lived here.

Then I realized he wasn't alone. Wrapped around him was his coworker, Lindsay. I'd never liked her. Her shirt flew through the air, hitting me in the face.

My mouth fell open. They crashed up against the wall next to the door, not even noticing my presence. At the same moment, I finished my drop. Unfortunately, I closed my legs a split second too late. My ass slammed into the ground. Ow.

Before I'd even finished registering the pain—much less processing everything else that happened—my phone started to ring. My best friend's ringtone.

"Not a good time, Lana," I muttered.

Finally, Gary and Lindsay realized they weren't alone. They looked over at me, still entwined. I couldn't stop staring at them. Couldn't speak. The room shrank until it contained nothing but them and me. And the incessant blaring of my ringtone. Lindsay's face.

Gary's voice broke into my stupor. "What are you doing here?"

"Me? What are you doing? And with her?" I jabbed a finger in Lindsay's direction. Last time we spoke, they were just friends. Although friends didn't text in the middle of the night.

"We thought you were at work," she said.

"Oh, well, that makes everything okay, doesn't it?" My voice rose with each word, reaching a pitch I'd never heard before. "How did you get in?"

"I used my key."

Something he certainly didn't get from me. "Why do you have a key?"

"I made a copy awhile back, in case I needed it for an emergency."

Closing my eyes, I forced myself to count to twenty before I answered. "Okay, Gary. Let's pretend that makes sense, although you should've told me. Why did you keep it after we broke up?"

He stuttered. Nothing he could say would make things better. My phone rang again. The sound pierced my brain like needles. Near hysteria, I grabbed the device from the tripod where I'd set it up.

Oh, no.

As soon as I got my hands on the phone, everything made sense. With a start, I realized exactly why my best friend kept calling me. The video was still recording. Posting on Facebook Live.

My routine.

Gary's entry. Making out with Lindsay.

My fall.

The revelation that my ex kept a copy of my key to use my house for sex. Ew. Ew. Ew. I needed a shower. And to change my locks.

But first, I needed to turn off my phone. Because as I stood frozen in horror, with all these thoughts reeling through my head, the reactions kept rolling by. Thumbs up. Laughing. Heart. Laughing.

~ I ~

The video went viral. Someone had managed to record it from their screen before I turned off the recording and deleted the file. Whoever it was shared on their page. So did everyone else in the world, it appeared. My friends were so used to sharing every pole fitness video they found with me that eleven of them posted it to my own wall with some version of "Haha! ZOMG this is hilarious!" before I shut down my page.

What a nightmare.

While waiting for the emergency all-night locksmith, I called my boss.

"Helen, I'm so sorry," I began before she could even say anything. "Hold on. Are you laughing?"

"Oh, Mel, you're brilliant!"

"I am?"

"Absolutely! That video is hilarious. Do you see how many views it's gotten?"

No, I did not. Because after I'd finally gotten Gary and Lindsay out of my house and deleted the post, I'd texted Lana to thank her for letting me know what was happening. She convinced me not to look at the numbers. Easy enough, since I didn't want to know how many strangers witnessed my humiliation.

"Um, a lot?"

"Thousands at least. I've watched it twelve times myself. I can't help it." Helen laughed, a high-pitched girlish sound that seemed foreign coming from a seventy-year-old woman. "This is amazing! The phones are ringing off the hook. I'm so glad you remembered to put the pitch for the studio at the beginning of the tape instead of waiting until the end."

"Yeah, you know Helen, that ending wasn't exactly what I'd planned—"

"Pfft. Oh, I'm sure it wasn't. But there's no such thing as bad publicity, dear. This is going to be amazing for the studio."

"You're not mad? Embarrassed for me?"

"Oh, I'm completely embarrassed for you. You must be horrified. What a way to get dumped."

"Actually, I dumped Gary six months ago."

"Shh, that's not what the viewers will see. It's okay, dear. If people feel sorry for you, they'll spend money on more classes. This is such a brilliant marketing ploy, I can't believe I didn't think of it myself. Well done!"

I sighed. If I didn't know better, I'd think Helen was the one to copy and share the video. She certainly seemed delighted about my public humiliation. But she also called Facebook Live "a tape" and couldn't reset the password on her smartphone. "Well, I'm glad I could help. I think."

"Don't worry," she said. "Come by the studio a little early tomorrow, and we can talk strategy. I know you're humiliated. But time heals all wounds. And so does extra pay. Everything will be fine."

"I guess that's good, then. I'll see you later."

We hung up. Despite my better judgment, I opened my laptop. The video didn't take long to find. Three more people had attempted to share it with me, and ten others tried to tag me. Some "friends" they were. I blocked the taggers, paused to greet the locksmith who knocked on my front door, then pulled the video up again.

I didn't want to see it. Even knowing that I needed to know to mitigate the damage—ignorance is truly bliss sometimes. The longer I hesitated, the less I wanted to see it.

Finally, with a deep breath, I forced my fingers to the "play" button.

There I was, dancing. Talking about how great pole was. And…. thud! Slamming into the floor. Oh, man. It was just as bad as I thought. Cringing, I covered my face with my hands. A soft moan escaped my lips.

"Hilarious, isn't it?" The locksmith's voice jolted me out of my self-pity.

"What?"

He gestured at the screen. "Sorry, I couldn't help but hear what you were listening to. That video. A friend sent it to me earlier. So funny. That woman sure got some surprise, didn't she?"

Yeah. Some surprise indeed.

"They're calling her The Fall Girl." The man leaned closer, peering at my face. "Hold on a sec…"

I stood and slammed the computer shut, then spun away from him. "I need to get some water. Is the lock almost done?"

"There's a pole in your living room… and that door. The locks!" If I'd listened any harder, I've had heard the light bulb going on in his head. "You're the Fall Girl! Dude, that rocks. I can't wait to tell my friends."

"You know, I'd really prefer you didn't."

Chortling, he banged his palms on my kitchen island. "Oh, the guys are never gonna believe this! Come on. Can I take a selfie with you?"

He wasn't going to let it go. He wasn't going to leave. Helen's words flashed through my head. *There's no such thing as bad publicity.*

After a minute, I sighed. "Fine. After the locks are changed."

# Chapter Two

**Hood Ornament:** You can get into this move from a basic or side climb. I prefer the side. Hook your inside knee around the pole and pull upward with your inside arm. Wrap your outside foot around the bottom of the pole and tuck the pole into your armpit. Put your arms straight out and tilt your head back. Don't point your toes until you've got the move down!

*- Push and Pole Fitness Tutorials, Vol. 2*

A block away from the studio the next afternoon, a fire engine passed, sirens blaring. Another fire truck passed. I watched it head off down the street, wondering if I should call Helen. There could be an emergency near the studio. Not a whiff of smoke in the air, though. Then a police car whizzed by before I even managed to pull back into traffic. That settled it. Time to call and see what was happening. Traffic was only getting worse ahead of me.

Helen didn't answer either the studio line or her cell phone, so I turned down a side street and took the back way into the studio's parking lot. Flashing lights at the other end of the alley made my pulse quicken, but I still didn't smell any smoke. Maybe something else had gone wrong—a water main break? Cat stuck in a tree?

Hopefully, whatever it was, the fire trucks wouldn't stop my students from getting to class. My pay depended on the number of people who showed up each week. The one bright side of that stupid video was the possibility of extra students. If they couldn't make it to the front door, most newbies wouldn't come back. Tomorrow, I'd be forgotten news.

My phone vibrated in my bag. Probably Helen returning my calls. As I dug for the device, my toe caught on something on the ground, and I went reeling forward. I swung my arms, stumbling to catch my balance. How graceful.

Falling flat on my face in public was exactly what I needed the day after, well—falling on my butt in public. Before I hit the ground, a pair of strong arms caught me. Embarrassed, I looked up into a pair of flawless blue eyes. The owner had narrow, pointed features like someone pinched the dough when molding his face. His brown hair was parted neatly on the side with a line so straight it could've been drawn with a ruler. There were all things I saw easily since I towered over him in my five-inch-heels. He also wore shoes so shiny I could see my face in them, which probably meant he had money. Or too much free time. Who got their shoes shined anymore?

"Whoa there. Are you okay?" he asked.

My face grew warm. Way to pay attention to my surroundings. "Sure. Sorry I wasn't looking where I was going."

"No problem. Happy to help." He studied my face while I held my breath.

*Please don't recognize me. Please please please.* While I ordinarily loved when people watched my videos, I did not want to be known as the teacher who fell off the pole.

His gaze lingered on my shoes. "Hold on. You're not going to the studio, are you?"

Something about the way he asked made me feel like honesty was not the best policy here. I clutched my coat closer around me, as if he could see through the layers of down to the glittery bra top and booty shorts beneath. Then I glanced at the shop adjacent to the parking lot. "Uh, no. I'm just getting a cup of coffee."

"Great! In that case, feel free to join us." He shoved a flyer into my hand before disappearing around the corner in the direction of Dance 4 U.

Weird, but I'd worry about it after class. My phone rang again, so I shoved the paper in my bag while rooting around to see who kept calling. Before I found the phone, I got to the end of the alley and, for the second time, I came to a dead halt.

A wall of people greeted me. For a split second, I thought some good had come out of my viral video, and everyone showed up to take my beginner pole fitness class. But one glance at the shirts buttoned to the chin and the pinched faces glaring at me told me I had another think coming.

Quietly, trying not to draw attention to myself, I sidled up to the nearest woman, leaning conspiratorially to whisper in her ear. "What's going on?"

"You won't believe what's happening," she said. "Did you know there is a stripper factory right here in our little town?"

I gasped in fake horror, trying to conceal a laugh. "I'm sorry. A what?"

"There's a woman here who teaches young, impressionable minds how to become strippers! Look, there's even a class for little kids!"

Of course. The new "mommy and me" class. Far from being a stripper class, the intent was to help women bond with their toddlers while getting into shape. Help the kids burn off some energy (and hopefully sleep after), while the moms rebuilt their core strength.

I took a deep breath. "That's not exactly what the classes are—"

"Hey! You! You're not welcome here!"

The man from the alley strode toward us, looking decidedly less friendly than he had a few minutes earlier. The crowd parted around him as if he were the Second Coming.

"Are you talking to me?" I asked, although the answer seemed rather obvious.

"I knew you looked familiar," he said. "I didn't recognize you with so many clothes on."

The dig made me roll my eyes, but I didn't bother to respond.

"What's wrong, Curtis?" the woman asked.

"I'll tell you what's wrong," the man, presumably Curtis, said. "The woman you're talking to is exactly who we're protesting here. She's the one teaching the stripper classes."

Putting my hands on my hips, I glared down at him. "I take it you're not here to sign up for lessons?"

"We're here to shut you down," he said. "We don't want your kind in our neighborhood. This is a Christian town, founded on Christian values."

"No, it isn't. This is Upstate New York. Saratoga Springs. We're known for horse racing, not religion. You have no right to shut me down."

He shrugged. "Maybe not yet. But we're working to pass an ordinance to ensure that people like you are forced to remain outside the city limits."

"How could you possibly do that?" I snorted. "I'm no lawyer, but I believe we're protected by a little thing like the First Amendment. Dancing is a type of expression."

"The First Amendment doesn't protect immoral activity."

A choking sound escaped me. "You've got to be kidding!

No one is going to agree to something like that. I'm a dance teacher. There's no 'immoral activity' going on here."

"Says you," he said. "But I'll have enough support to put it to a vote. And after the election, I'll be able to use my connections to get the city council on board."

I shook my head. Why hadn't I heard about any of this? "You're holding an election to shut down the dance studio?"

"Don't be ridiculous. I can't do that."

"That's the first thing you've said that makes any sense."

"The election is to fill the vacant state senate seat," he said impatiently. "Don't tell me you're the only person in Saratoga County who didn't hear the news."

I wracked my brain, but I'd never cared in the slightest about state politics. If this rando hadn't blocked my entrance to work, I wouldn't care now. "Sorry. Drawing a blank."

"Tiberius Baker's seat is open," the woman beside me said helpfully.

He rolled his eyes. "I shouldn't have expected any better of you."

"So what happened to good 'ole Tiberius?"

"My father resigned his seat," Curtis sniffed, as if relaying this news was beneath him. "He had an 'epiphany'."

Okay, whatever that meant. I'd barely paid attention to local news recently, and I didn't have time to get any deeper into this conversation. My students would be waiting inside. Assuming they managed to wade through the throng of people in the street.

"Your father sounds like a swell guy," I said. "If he shares your views, we're better off without him in politics. I can't wait to donate to your opponent. Now, if you'll excuse me, I have a class to teach."

With as much dignity as I could muster, I swept around him and began to glide through the crowd toward the front door.

"Enjoy your class!" He yelled behind me. I gave him the finger. "It'll be your last. After I'm elected, you'll have to keep your clothes on!"

Forcing myself not to shake with rage, I kept my head high as I walked into the building, letting the door slam shut behind me.

What a jerk. I couldn't believe his nerve. It wasn't enough that he judged what I did, but now he was trying to physically prevent me from doing it? I'd thought New York was supposed to be a fairly liberal state, but there were apparently pushy-nose-in-your-business types everywhere.

The clock on the wall ticked loudly, reminding me that I couldn't sit here and fume all day. In less than ten minutes, my first class of the day would arrive. Taking a deep breath, I moved around my studio, allowing it to calm me the way it always did. The only thing better than this place would be when I opened my own business, teaching on my terms. Where, among other things, my boss wouldn't be delighted when I accidentally humiliated myself.

In a few short minutes, the room would come alive with activity. Now, fairy lights twinkled in the silence. The mirrors on the walls gleamed, and the poles waited. This was my favorite part of the day. I savored the silence, running through the evening's lesson in my head.

Meanwhile, my body went through the mechanics of my favorite moves. Up, down, around. Far too advanced for tonight's beginner class, but these spins and holds put me in the zone.

A ding from my phone brought me back into the moment. Showtime.

Slowly, I lowered myself to the floor, inch by inch, stretching out my legs. Then I went to open the door and greet my students. Thankfully, the mess outside hadn't prevented them from getting to the door.

They filed in, the newbies huddling in the corner near the cubbies with their doe eyes while those who'd been here before knew what to do. I directed the new students to take off their shoes and line up. When they finished, I faced them with a smile.

"Welcome! I'm Mel. I've been teaching for about eight years now, and I'm here to tell you, this is the best type of workout."

"Are you a stripper?"

Used to the question, I smiled gently at the person who asked. "I'm not, but strippers pioneered this sport. In this room, strippers are our muses, our inspiration. We get enough slut-shaming out in the world." Like from those idiots outside, I didn't say.

Her face reddened, and I grasped the instructor pole at the front of the room to draw attention away from her. I slid smoothly to the floor, then back up, giving bedroom eyes while still talking. "Pole can be whatever you need it to be. You can be sexy if you want. You don't have to."

With my left hand, I gripped the pole at knee level. My right hand grabbed the pole above my head. Slowly, I lifted my body off the floor, my legs and arms creating an X. One of the girls gasped. Others clapped. "For some people, pole is about strength. That's why I got started. Some people like the tricks. Don't worry. We'll start with some simple spins and stretches. No advanced moves this week."

One of the more advanced beginner students snorted. She knew the move I'd just shown them took years of training. I caught her eye and grinned.

"Okay! Let's start with a basic warm-up."

Music filled the room. In unison, six women of all ages, shapes, and sizes followed as I led them through the motions, following a warm-up routine so familiar I could do it in my sleep. Had done it with pneumonia.

About halfway through the class, the door swung open. Helen stuck her head in. Worry lined her face. Helen had been a dancer for about sixty years, and she looked it. Solid muscle from head to toe, long gray hair always pulled back in a bun, dark eyes that usually danced with her *joie de vivre*. She wore tights and flowy skirts and leotards, whether she taught ballet or salsa or the waltz. The one thing she never, ever taught was pole. She never entered this room once that door closed at the start of my classes.

Concerned, I told the students to keep practicing and hustled over her. She motioned me into the lobby, not speaking until the door shut behind me. The music from the stereo stopped abruptly.

"I'm so sorry, Mel. I hate to do this. We have to cancel your classes."

"What? Why?" My stomach twisted. This couldn't be a coincidence. It had to be related to Curtis and his crowd of fools.

"I guess I shouldn't have been so flippant about negative publicity." She held a piece of paper out to me, her face white. "They got an emergency temporary injunction. We've been shut down."

# Chapter Three

**Spinning Swan**: This is a great move for exhibitions, because it looks a lot more difficult than it is, and it's very pretty. Don't attempt on a static/locked pole; you'll just be a sitting swan.

*- Push and Pole Fitness Tutorials, Vol. 1*

Helen's words rang in my ears the entire time I cleaned out my locker. Her voice haunted me down the stairs and out of the studio. *Shut down…no job…they think we're a "bad influence on the community."*

I fumed. Who did that Curtis jerk think he was? Who made him the morality police? He was probably one of those guys who thought it was women's fault he couldn't control his libido. That wearing a short skirt or dancing around in a skimpy outfit (aka a dance costume) was "asking for it."

I'd begged my boss to let me work until the injunction lifted, but she'd said she couldn't risk more bad exposure. If the morality police outside realized that I was still in there, working, planning to start teaching again, they might never go away. If they made her other students leave, or worse got a more expansive injunction, she could lose the business she'd spent decades building. All because some people felt that their personal definition of morality should be allowed to dictate other people's behavior.

Although I understood why Helen couldn't keep me on, it hurt. What was I going to do now? Pole fitness studios weren't exactly like Zumba. I couldn't go to any local gym and sign up to teach. At a minimum, the owner of the space would have to pay several hundred dollars to install poles and buy mats. Worse, any local studio that did a basic search for my name would find both the disaster video and the injunction. They wouldn't be jumping at the change to invest in me.

My throat tightened at the thought. For a minute, I couldn't breathe. I stopped and forced myself to inhale and exhale slowly. This wasn't the time to be upset. If anyone from the protest lingered outside, I couldn't let them see me cry. Blinking away my tears, I threw open the front door.

With my head held high, I strutted down the street, away from the studio. Once around the corner and out of sight, I stopped, leaning against the side of a building. Don't cry. Don't cry. I took long, slow deep breaths, reminding myself that there were plenty of other dance studios in the Capital District. My students would follow me if I went somewhere else. But that didn't help if Curtis managed to pass a law that prevented me from teaching anywhere. Could he do that? Wouldn't the sheer number of representatives from New York City vote it down? There had to be a lot of them.

All of these thoughts swirled around in my head, making it difficult to focus on anything. Several long moments passed before I composed myself. My mind continued to race.

What was I going to do? Helen might let me come back once her lawyers got the injunction lifted, but that didn't help me if Curtis got the laws changed. Could he do that? I had no idea. Besides, I wasn't sure I wanted to go back to work for someone who cut me loose because of something that wasn't my fault. She could've let me answer phones, teach some of the yoga classes, anything.

It killed me that she'd cut me off so easily. I was the one who showed up on her doorstep and talked her into offering pole fitness lessons a few years ago. She'd never even heard of it. My classes made her a lot of money. Until they didn't. Now she had no use for me.

Sometimes I gave private lessons at home for extra cash and convenience, but my condo wasn't nearly big enough to teach more than one person at a time. I needed to find a new space ASAP—but what if Curtis got another temporary injunction against a different studio? How wide-reaching was his crusade? Could I go to Albany and teach there? It was about half an hour away, so kind of a pain, but not impossible if I found a space near the northern end. They had a pretty big college there. Maybe I could offer some student specials.

My blood boiled. I couldn't even get into my car to drive home without fear of running into something. Unfortunately, I couldn't stand out here all night, or I'd freeze. Going back inside wasn't an option, so I set off down the street. A brisk walk would burn off some frustration. Maybe if that Puritan asshole was still around, I could find him and punch him in the nose.

A headline swam before my eyes "Stripper Assaults Upstanding Citizen." Okay, fine, I wouldn't hit him. But I certainly would dream about it.

After a couple of turns around the block, I felt well enough to pause in my march of rage, so I stopped in at the coffee shop adjacent to the studio. Then I texted Lana that I'd be bringing over some tea and pastries for an emergency girls' night. Usually I preferred coffee, but at the moment I needed something to help lower my blood pressure. Coffee would make me tense, and if my nerves grew any more rigid, they might snap in half.

While I waited, I texted my students to let them know that my classes were canceled until further notice, but I'd be giving private lessons in my condo. Despite it being a Friday night, most of them wrote back immediately expressing outrage and support, which helped a little. By the time I collected my order and headed to the parking lot, I felt much better. I'd figure something out.

Outside, a guy who'd parked a bit too close to the edge of the lot struggled to dig his car out of the frozen mess. Silly. You never park next to the mountain of plowed snow unless you have four-wheel drive. You definitely don't park *on top* of it. Especially not when the snow is frozen solid, and you're wearing a thousand-dollar suit. He looked so pitiful that I went over to offer help.

This winter had been particularly swear-worthy, with Mother Nature dumping almost a foot of white powder like clockwork every Wednesday. Naturally, the temperature never rose enough to melt the snow, so after a couple of months of this, grimy white towers lined the sidewalks and created a perimeter around most public parking lots. People who didn't choose their spaces carefully risked getting stuck. Much like this guy.

At the sound of my feet crunching on the snow, he looked up. The guy was solid, muscular, and a few inches taller than me, making him probably around six-foot-three. The shape of his forearms told me he worked out regularly. He looked a little older than me, maybe early thirties. He had gorgeous, longish red hair, laughing hazel eyes, and a smattering of freckles across his nose. He was also very good-looking. I was such a sucker for freckles. When he spotted me, his smile lit up the gloomy day.

"Need help?" I asked.

His eyes swept the puffy coat and mittens covering my muscular frame. No one looked particularly strong when wearing layers of down. I braced myself, waiting for him to say something chauvinistic so I could tell him to go screw himself and continue to Lana's. After the day I'd had, I didn't really need another run-in, so I probably should have just gotten in my car and driven away without a word. But then he nodded.

"I'm completely stuck," he said. "I push the shovel as hard as I can, but it doesn't go anywhere. I guess that's what I get for driving a Smart Car in a New York winter."

I reached out with one hand. "May I?"

"I appreciate the offer, but are you sure you want to shovel snow in those shoes?"

Right. Six-inch pole platforms weren't ideal winter wear. But the ground wasn't icy, and at this point the shoes were practically extensions of my feet. "Eh. They're not my best pair."

He looked skeptical, but to his credit, he simply shrugged and took the tray of drinks from my hand before handing me the shovel. "Thanks."

Despite having a lot of strength and barely contained rage, turned out, my shoveling skills weren't all that superior to the car owner's. After a couple of minutes, I admitted defeat and stepped back, surveying the problem. He'd driven right up into the snowbank. The snow beneath the car lifted it off the ground, preventing the wheels on the passenger side from touching at all. Even if he stepped on the gas, no amount of shoveling or salt was going to help unless we got the car off that snow.

I moved around to the front license plate and put my hands on the hood. "Get in and put it in neutral."

"What are you going to do?"

"You're stuck on a mound of snow. I'm going to shove you off."

"You can't move a car!"

I thought about telling him that if I could hang upside-down in mid-air by one ankle, I could do anything, but it wasn't worth the questions such a statement usually inspired. I'd had enough negative attention for one night.

Instead I shrugged and crouched. "What have you got to lose?"

"If you accidentally kill yourself, I would feel terrible."

I grinned up at him. "I'll do my best to survive."

With another glance at me, he got in the car. A moment later, the parking brake disengaged, and the car engine revved. Through the windshield, he gave me a thumbs up. I braced myself against the snow at my back, dug my heels into the ice as well as I could, and shoved, praying the car wouldn't rocket backward into the vehicle behind it.

Of course it did.

He had been so skeptical I could move the car at all, he hadn't mentioned the consequence of pushing *too* hard. Meanwhile, in my haste to prove I was stronger than he thought, I may have gotten a bit overzealous. The tiny red car shot backward across the lane, which was thankfully free of oncoming traffic. It stopped with a thump when the rear bumper collided with my green Toyota Corolla, coming to rest in a circle of light provided by the street lamp.

A popping sound filled the air. Bits of red glass peppered the ground between our cars.

"Oops."

Inside the car, the man's face turned beet red. His shoulders shook. It took me a minute to realize he was laughing. He tumbled out of the driver's door, leaning against the side of the car for support while he got himself under control. Hesitantly, I walked toward him.

"Thank you?" he said. "I guess I should've believed you could help. But now I've got to leave a note for the owner of this car."

Sheepishly, I raised my hand. "Hi. Car owner, right here."

He laughed harder. Finally seeing the humor in the whole thing, I let out a giggle of my own. Before I knew it, the two of us were sitting on the ground in the snow, rocking back and forth, until an employee came out to see if we were okay. Wiping tears from our eyes, we sent her back inside.

"Listen, I have to get going," my new friend said. With a start, I realized that I didn't even know his name. It felt weird to ask now. Although theoretically, it would get weirder if we went out and got married and had beautiful kids and I still didn't know his name.

He got to his feet, brushing snow off the back of his coat before reaching down to help me up.

"Thanks," I said.

"No problem." He fished a business card out of his wallet and handed it to me. "For one thing, I made you break your taillight. Give me a call when you get it fixed, if not before."

"Thanks," I said absently.

A broken taillight for a fifteen-year-old car cost about twenty bucks to replace. I didn't need his help, not when it was entirely my fault. He was cute, though, so maybe it would be worth calling him in a couple of days, once I got my life sorted.

After I got into my car, I allowed myself one wistful glance into the rearview mirror. The guy still stood behind my car, waiting. I turned the key. As soon as my engine roared to life, he got into his own vehicle. What a gentleman. Waiting to make sure I was okay before taking off.

I watched him go, telling myself that I needed to let the car heat up before driving away. But I just wanted to keep him in sight as long as possible.

Finally, I let out a sigh, tossed his business card into my back seat, and shifted into gear.

~ I ~

**H**alf an hour later, I sat ensconced on my best friend's couch, buried under an afghan and balancing a tray of pastries on the seat between us. She remained perfectly silent as I told her the details of my night, from the mob waiting outside the dance studio until Helen burst into my class holding that stupid piece of paper.

The cute guy in the parking lot could wait for another day, so I tucked that part of the story away. Since it amounted to nothing but a bit of harmless flirting, there was no point in reliving those sparkling brown eyes. Hazel? The muscular fore-arms. The…

Nope. Not going there. Not now, anyway. We had more important things to talk about.

"Man, that sucks!" Lana said when I told her about the injunction. "What are you going to do?"

I sighed. "I have no idea. The only other pole studios around are at least an hour south of here. Or worse, all the way down in New York City. Who knows if anyone is hiring? And I don't want to drive all over the state to give a few classes here and there."

"Why work for someone else? You've got loyal students who would follow you anywhere, but we'd rather travel to Ball-ston Spa or Saratoga Springs than trek ninety minutes each way for a one-hour class. Even me, and you know how much I love you."

"You think I should open my own studio?"

"Why not? You could make way more working for yourself than someone else. Helen was delighted by your public humiliation. She fired you over something that wasn't remotely your fault. Do you want to risk working for someone else like that? As your own boss, you can make the studio look the way you want, advertise, get the word out—and keep all the profits."

With each word Lana spoke, I grew more excited. "That's true. Most of my students should stick with me, as long as I can get up and running soon."

"You were never thrilled with that space anyway, right?"

Helen's studio had low ceilings and limited space, not much light, and was stifling in the summer. Still the hours were flexible, and she'd given me a good break when I started. We got along well.

Diplomatically, I said, "It wasn't ideal."

"Picture this," Lana said. "A studio with an entire room full of poles, so eight or nine people can work out all at once. No sharing. No spending half the class waiting to take your turn. Twenty-foot ceilings. A studio where you're not fighting for space with Zumba in the mornings and foxtrot classes at night. One with a cleaning lady so you don't have to spend hours each week vacuuming and wiping down the mirrors."

My hopes continued to rise. The more Lana talked, the more perfect her solution sounded. I'd been wondering if I should relocate for a while now: every time it rained, I had to put buckets in the ladies' room to catch the water dripping from the ceiling. The Push and Pole name belonged to me, even though the business operated out of Dance 4 U. I could take it anywhere.

Creating my dream studio could be expensive, but I had a little money saved to help pay my bills until I started to turn a profit. My parents might help if I asked them to. Things started to come together in my mind. I could do this.

"You're right, Lana," I said. "But how am I going to pay for all that? Take out second a mortgage on my condo?"

"Don't do that. Although I have absolute faith in you, small businesses don't always do well. There are outside factors in play. If this Curtis guy follows you to your new location, you could be in a position to lose your home, and that's not going to happen."

Just like that, my bubble burst. "Well, it was a nice dream for a few seconds."

"Shush. You can still do this. I'll help you apply for a small business loan."

"And if Curtis passes a law banning pole fitness studios?"

"One newbie state senator doesn't have that kind of power."

"He made it sound like he's got contacts. Apparently, his dad used to be in the seat. We have no idea what kind of support he might be able to drum up, especially after that stupid video." I sighed. "You didn't see the crowd of protestors outside the studio."

"It'll be okay," she said. "One thing at a time. Start looking for another job. But also see if you can find your own space. We'll manage everything else as it comes up."

It wasn't a perfect plan, but it was the best we had at the moment.

Before I did anything else, I emailed several fitness studio owners in other counties to see if anyone wanted to offer pole classes. Then I messaged every pole instructor I knew in the state, a couple in Massachusetts and Vermont, and a few strip clubs, to see if anyone knew a place hiring an instructor.

Lana's idea still appealed to me, but I needed to be realistic. You didn't start a business on a whim with no capital and no investors. I had bills to pay, and it took time to get a business off the ground. A small business loan sounded great, but I'd need income to make the monthly payments. And to eat. Pay my mortgage. Lana was right: risking my home made no sense.

On the other hand, I did have a healthy list of students in the Saratoga area who would probably follow me to a new studio. Especially since Helen no longer offered pole fitness classes for the foreseeable future.

Not quite ready to give up yet, I surfed commercial real estate for rent in the nearby counties, looking for the right space. I just needed a plan. With higher ceilings, I could offer aerial yoga or Lyra classes, too. There was plenty of time to get certified once I got up and running. Pole muscles and flexibility translated to plenty of other activities, so it shouldn't be a problem. Or I could advertise for another instructor, find someone to share the load.

Lana had the skills, and she'd be a great business partner, but seemed unlikely to give up practicing law for fitness instruction. It didn't pay quite the same. Too bad, because she always seemed twice as alive doing pole as talking about work.

Things to worry about tomorrow, I decided. For now, bed. With dreams of laughing hazel eyes and scattered freckles dancing in my head.

# Chapter Four

**Star Gazer:** Start from a basic climb. Wrap your top leg around the pole, securing it in your knee pit. Hold your top leg securely with one hand, then lean back, looking up toward the ceiling. Simple, yet beautiful.

*- Push and Pole Fitness Tutorials, Vol, 2*

Saturday mornings at Dance 4 U were the highlight of my week. Students flooded the waiting area, chatting excitedly. I usually arrived early enough to open the room and get the heat going, then wandered around talking to some of the regulars who I saw all the time. A couple of times a month, I did bachelorette parties or birthday parties or whatever. Once I did an adoption shower, which was a lot of fun. Even better when both spouses or both parents joined in.

But no more. I woke up the next morning to the sounds of my upstairs neighbors chattering and banging away in their kitchen, no doubt making some amazing family breakfast. The scents of bacon and eggs caused me to inhale deeply, my mouth watering.

Having an unexpected day at home just made me feel like I'd put my clothes on backward or something. The day stretched before me, empty and confusing. I didn't know what to do with myself. Time crawled.

After doing all the laundry that I'd allowed to build up over time, making my own breakfast, sanitizing every surface Gary had touched when he burst in, and throwing dinner in the slow cooker, I checked my phone: not even ten o'clock yet. Lovely.

Driving to the auto parts store and replacing my tail light took up half an hour, but I was officially at loose ends. I wasn't great at relaxing. I tried to do a pole workout, but that just made me sad. Finally I plopped down with my tablet and started making a list of places I could probably get a job, even if I couldn't teach pole.

By one o'clock, I was thinking about reorganizing my sock drawer. Finally, I gave into temptation and opened a new web browser. The name was burned into my memory, so it only took a moment before a page of results filled my screen.

Like he mentioned last night, Curtis Baker was the son of Tiberius Baker. I recognized the name as belonging to a local politician, but also from the conversation. Every couple of years for as long as I could remember, the "Vote for Baker" signs peppered the area. I'd never voted for him, but he'd won a bunch of times. He was always on the ballot as the incumbent. Too bad. In 2018, I'd really liked his opponent.

Baker apparently went to a lot of events with his son. The two of them appeared in one photo after another: campaigning together, fund-raising together, feeding the homeless together. One caption explained why: Curtis was Baker's campaign manager in election years and Chief of Staff all the time. Too bad. He was in a position to know what the residents wanted, and I hated to think they wanted to take women's rights back about fifty years.

Something caught my eye as I scrolled, and I halted. According to this, Senator Baker experienced a heart attack while playing tennis a couple of weeks ago. Although in his early sixties, the senator exercised daily, ate a healthy diet, never smoked or drank. He recovered quickly, but the experience reportedly shook him to the core. He sold all of his possessions, bought a used RV, moved into it with the family's housekeeper, and... started selling skincare products? That couldn't be right. From the state senate to operating a multilevel marketing scheme out of a motorhome?

Right or wrong, Baker's resignation shocked everyone who knew him (according to the newspaper). It also left a vacancy in the state senate. They were holding a special election in a couple of months. And who was running but the former senator's oldest son/campaign manager/chief of staff.

Well, that explained why Curtis was coming after me with his family values crap now. He probably thought it would win him back voters who didn't approve of his father's behavior. Not my vote, but maybe someone's. The district had been voting red for decades, so it must be more conservative than I thought. I couldn't wait to donate to Curtis's opponent, just like I told him. I may not have a lot of money, but every bit helped. Or I could donate time, of which I suddenly had plenty.

Opening another tab, I started typing. No results. I checked again. Then again. Nothing. Finally, I texted Lana.

*Hey, what would I do if I wanted to know who was running for office?*

*Take your temperature,* she replied.

*Very funny,* I typed.

Quickly I explained why I asked. My laundry buzzed, and by the time I finished switching everything over, two more texts awaited me. Looked like good 'ole Curtis was currently running unopposed. Meaning that bastard would soon be a member of the state legislature. I groaned.

Realizing that this conversation would be much easier to have verbally, I tapped on Lana's name to call her.

"You're sure no one is running against Curtis?"

"Pretty sure," she said. "The filing deadline is Monday, so theoretically someone else could put their name in. But I'm not finding anything that suggests anyone is even planning to run."

"What about that guy who ran a few years ago? He was in all the papers. Marlow Wright? I feel like I see that guy's name everywhere. People love him."

"That's because he's the state Attorney General now."

Oh. Right. "Do you think he'd want to–?"

She laughed. "No. Look, I've got a friend who works for the local Democratic Committee. I'll give him a call, but he may not get back to me on a Saturday."

"Tell him I want to give them money. That usually helps." I paused. "Wait. I don't have any money. Tell him I'll volunteer for the campaign. Going door-to-door, handing out flyers, making phone calls, whatever."

"I have a sneaking suspicion there isn't anyone to volunteer for," she said. "But I'll pass it on."

"Thanks, Lana. You're the best."

Another alert popped up on my phone, this one from my public Facebook page. With everything that happened, I hadn't thought to close it down yet, and someone was inquiring about a party.

With a pang I realized that the injunction not only stopped me from teaching classes, it meant I couldn't schedule any parties or special events for the foreseeable future. Helen's studio was unavailable, and my living room just wasn't big enough. I loved those events, both because they allowed me to meet new people and because they usually resulted in new business.

New business I could no longer use without a place to teach them.

Stupid Curtis Baker.

Just as I started to relieve my frustration by writing an email that I would never send, my phone beeped with another text from Lana.

My heart sank as I read it. *They don't have anyone.*

*That's it? They're giving up?*

*Daniel didn't sound happy about it*, she replied. *Asked if I wanted to run. Or if you did. ;-)*

My laughter filled the room. As if. Why stop there? Why not run for president?

But then my eyes landed on the copy of the injunction Helen had printed, sitting on the island. I'd brought it home to read, although nothing it said made me feel any better. Even if I'd understood half the language used, just the court caption at the top of the page made my blood boil all over again.

Curtis Baker was a spoiled jerk, a guy who'd had everything handed to him his whole life. Rich father, expensive education, flashy watch. Clothes worth more than my car. He walked with a swagger, spoke like someone used to getting what they wanted. Now he managed to cancel my business, to take a huge chunk of Helen's income, and he wanted to go even further. He wanted to stop me from teaching pole anywhere in this community. If he got into the Legislature, it would be that much harder to stop him.

No.

My whole life, I'd had things taken away from me. My dad was in the military, so we constantly moved. Each time, I had to leave all my friends behind, learn to fit in somewhere new. All through high school, it had been impossible to let down my guard enough to date because of the fear that we'd get sent somewhere else. Signing the papers to buy my condo had been one of the most exciting moments of my life. It meant finally knowing that I wouldn't have to move again.

If I couldn't teach, I couldn't pay my mortgage. I wasn't about to give up my livelihood without a fight. At only twenty-eight years old, I'd started over more than most people did in a lifetime. Now, I wanted to hold onto my roots.

Before I could reconsider, I snatched up my phone and texted back. *Give me Daniel's number. I'm in.*

# Chapter Five

**Cocoon:** Until you get the hang of this move, you'll want a spotter or a crash mat. Or both. Essentially, once you're hanging upside-down by your inside leg, you're going to pull your outside leg and arch your back to bring foot and head together…

*- Push and Pole Fitness Tutorials, Vol. 4*

My bravado faded slightly by the time I arrived at Daniel's office to talk about my rash decision. Who was I to run for office?

A New York resident, I told myself firmly. A valuable member of the Saratoga community.

A strong, innovative woman with ideas about how to better the lives of the people in her area. Or at least make it a little more tolerant.

I had a right to a better future for myself and my neighbors. No, an obligation. Even if I lost spectacularly—which seemed likely—at least I didn't sit back and let other people make decisions for me.

Before I could talk myself out of this meeting, I knocked on the closed door. It swung open as my inner debate raged on.

My first sight of this political advisor stopped me in my tracks. For some reason, I'd been prepared to meet with, well, basically Leo from *The West Wing:* older, reserved, somewhat unfriendly, in an expensive suit. Instead, I found myself face-to-face with the gorgeous freckles and smile that I'd met last night while pushing his car out of the snow.

He looked more well-rested, and he wore old blue jeans and a dark green polo shirt instead of the suit he'd had on before. But it was definitely him. The guy whose name I'd stupidly never gotten.

"Hey. Are you here about the car?" He eyed me warily, like he was wondering if he needed to call and request a restraining order. After all, showing up at someone's place of business to talk about a busted taillight was creepy. Especially because, you know, it was entirely my fault.

"No, not at all. This is so weird." He still looked confused, so I put out my hand to shake. "I'm Mel Martin. Lana's friend."

His eyes widened. "Daniel O'Brien. It's nice to meet you. Small world, huh?"

"Tiny. That coffee shop is next to my dance studio. Do you go there a lot?"

He shook his head. "Never. I was at the protest, keeping an eye on things. It's good to see you, though. I was sure I'd never hear from you."

"You were right," I admitted. "Just… I mean, I can pay for the taillight myself. I should be paying to fix your car."

"Don't be ridiculous. You did me a favor. Without you, I'd have needed to call for a tow." With a start, he realized that we still stood in the doorway of his office. "I'm sorry. Come in, come in. Let's talk."

The office was small, but Daniel utilized the space well. Shelves and filing cabinets filled the walls. A large desk took up most of the center of the room, with papers stacked on every available surface. All perfectly arranged. I'd bet I could ask him for any paper in those stacks, and he would have it in hand within seconds. Meanwhile, I needed GPS to find a clean sports bra in the morning.

Daniel directed me to the chair facing his desk and offered me coffee. Too much caffeine made me jittery, and I was nervous enough, so I declined. He settled into his seat without making his own cup. "So Lana tells me you want to run for our vacant seat. Can I ask why?"

"I don't like Curtis Baker."

He laughed, a loud, booming sound that put me at ease. Politics didn't have to be scary and stiff and formal. "Direct and to the point. I like that. If you're running for office, you may need to learn to be less candid."

"Do I have to pretend to like him?"

"No. I can't say that you do."

"Then we'll be fine." I explained what happened Friday night and how that fed into my decision to run. "Originally I just wanted to volunteer to help his opponent, but Lana said there's no one running."

Daniel listened without comment, taking the occasional note on a legal pad in front of him. "That's unfortunately true. This has been a red district for a long time. I've been trying to find a new candidate for ages. Almost had someone lined up, but he fell through. And I thought there would be more time."

"Yeah, I read about that. I can't believe Senator Baker just up and walked out." No point mentioning that I found the article roughly three hours ago, rather than when it happened. "Well, Former Senator, I guess."

"I hate that you got caught up in all this. Baker Senior's move is why Curtis is pushing the family values things so much. I doubt he believes half of it, but his mom was devastated when his father left her for a much younger woman. It's such a cliché. Curtis is trying to repair the family name."

"What about you? You're smart, you're employed by the party so you must be dedicated, you've got experience with politics. Why don't you run?"

"Unfortunately, I don't live in the district," he said. "The open seat covers the area from Saratoga Springs, where you have your studio, north toward some of the more rural areas, and east. I live further south, closer to Albany."

"That sucks. Want to move?"

He snorted. "Thanks, but no. I like my job. I'm good at helping things run smoothly behind the scenes. Running for office isn't for me."

Too bad. In the last major election, people went on and on about "not liking" one candidate or the other. I'd met Daniel less than twenty-four hours ago, and I already liked him way more than Curtis. Of course, the bar was low.

"So, that's it? I can run?"

"Do you have any relevant political experience? Anything that would help us show you're the right person for the job?"

"I'm friendly, I'm hard-working, I'm driven. Isn't the beauty of the American system that anyone can pull themselves up by their strappy high-heels and become someone?"

"Let's hold off before making that our campaign slogan." He smiled at me, and I wondered if he was remembering the heels I wore when we met. "But you have a point. Go on."

"I'm good with people. That's what makes me a great teacher. I explain things in a way that makes sense, which should help when talking about the issues." I took a deep breath. "And if all that's not enough, this might be a good time to mention that I have a bachelor's degree in Political Science."

He raised his eyebrows at me. "Oh, yeah? What happened?"

I shrugged. "I needed a job. I got really into pole in college. I mean—pole fitness, not polls like elections."

Daniel chuckled. "Right. Go on."

"When an instructor job opened up, teaching seemed more fun than putting on a suit every day. Is that enough? It sounds like I'm your only option."

"You are, actually. But I'm not sure it's that easy," Daniel said.

My hopes deflated a bit. "Why not?"

"I'm not sure how to put this delicately." He cleared his throat. "Please don't take this the wrong way. I like you, Mel. You seem intelligent, you know how to go after what you want, and you're passionate."

"Why do I feel a 'but' coming on?" Leaning back, I crossed my arms over my chest and braced for the impact of whatever he said next.

"Because you're also perceptive." Our eyes met, and for a heartbeat, I got the feeling Daniel wished we'd met anywhere else. Maybe that was my own wishful thinking. "People think Saratoga Springs is liberal because we've got the women's college, the fancy coffee houses, the row of shops."

"Don't forget the indie bookstore."

"Never." He paused, and his face grew serious. "But the area as a whole tends to be pretty conservative. We've got old money here, the horse racing, the history—and that tends to make people predisposed to buy into Curtis's whole 'Make Saratoga Moral Again' thing."

"Please tell me that's not actually his slogan."

He shrugged. "At the moment, he doesn't need a slogan. With no one else on the ballot, the only vote he needs to win is his. Presumably, his mother and partner will also vote for him, so it'll be 3-0."

"Hold on," I said. "The Republican family values candidate is gay?"

Daniel grimaced. "Sorry, I shouldn't have said that. It's not common knowledge, but I've known Curtis since college, when he didn't feel the need to hide. Please don't say anything."

"I wouldn't out him. That's not me. It's just…he wants to pass laws stopping pole," I said. "Not just in Saratoga, but statewide. He thinks he can use his connections to take away people's livelihoods, all in the name of morality."

"He said that?"

"He did," I said.

Daniel sighed. "That does present a problem. If he wins, his party will have a majority. As much as it's obviously a terrible law, and likely unconstitutional, he may be able to convince people to vote for it out of misplaced loyalty. It takes time to get garbage laws overturned by the courts, and the people who pass them know it."

"That's what I'm afraid of. He's already shut me down, and made my boss cancel a bunch of classes," I said. "I can't let him go after anyone else. What he's doing is wrong."

"You're right," Daniel said finally.

"Can I run?"

"I want to say yes. Very badly."

"So say it. What's stopping you?"

He hesitated. "I hate to say it, but the problem, Ms. Martin, is you. More specifically, what you do for a living."

"Oh." The same reason Curtis wanted to shut me down. I swallowed back a wave of disappointment. I shouldn't have even come here in the first place. What a stupid idea. That spark between us must've been my imagination. "So that's it then? I'm wasting my time?"

"I'm not saying that. The party would love to win this seat back. They'd be thrilled with me if I managed to find a winning candidate. But we do need to take care in how we present you to the public. New York is a fairly liberal state over-all, but this district extends up into more conservative areas. Maybe your job wouldn't matter in the City. It matters here."

"Why? Melania Trump used to do nude modeling, and no one cared." It barely even came up during the election, probably because there were a couple dozen other reasons not to vote for her husband.

Daniel said, "Trump was already well-known. He had fans. But frankly, there's always been a double standard with Republicans excusing behavior in their own that they won't tolerate in a Democrat."

Argh. He was right. I couldn't court the homophobic vote, even if I wanted to. And I knew for a fact the towns north of us were more conservative than mine: Last time I checked, not a single pole fitness studio could be found in that part of the state—or, really, anywhere between Saratoga County and the Canadian border.

The impact of Daniel's words nauseated me: I could be out of the race before I even started, just because I took pride in my body. But still, I was proud of who I was and what I'd accomplished in life. Curtis couldn't take that away from me.

"I can do this. I can run, and I can win." Steel entered my spine, and I glared at him without blinking. "Without changing who I am."

"I'm not asking you to," Daniel said. "You've got a fire that we could use in the legislature. It's a constant battle to move our agenda, with the other side stopping us at every turn. I love your passion. But you will have to make some changes."

Changes? For a moment, I wonder if I'd made a mistake in coming here. The whole point of stopping Curtis was to avoid having to change. "What did you have in mind?"

"To start, don't post any more videos," he said, "at least not until this is over."

"Deal. My bum still hurts from the last one."

"We're going to need to figure out how to deal with your occupation, convince the voters that it's not a bad thing." He glanced down at my glittery shoes and leggings. "Do you have a professional wardrobe?"

My gaze followed his, and my cheeks burned. I probably should've made more of an effort to look like a senator (or at least a candidate) before coming here. "No, I'm afraid not."

"That gives us a starting point," Daniel said. "First, we'll hire an image consultant. Someone who can teach you things like how to talk to the press. Help you pick out a conservative wardrobe for events, things like that."

"That sounds expensive," I said slowly. "I want to do this, but I don't have a lot of money. If I'm buying business clothes and stuff, that's fine. I'll use them. But what does an image consultant cost?"

"Don't worry about it."

"I have to worry about it. I'm an out-of-work pole fitness instructor with an injunction against getting a new job."

"Sorry, that's not what I meant," Daniel said. "The party really wants this seat back. There are some important bills coming up in the next few months, and one vote could make the difference. We've been raising money for months, grooming a candidate to go against Baker. Our pick had to drop out, but we've still got some money available to throw behind you."

"In that case, I'm in," I said. "Just tell me what you need me to do—my schedule is completely clear."

"Excellent! Let's take things one day at a time. I'll have an image consultant contact you. I know the perfect person. She used to work in the First Lady's press office. She has a brilliant political mind and a degree in public relations, plus extensive experience in D.C. before she moved to the area."

"You can't do it?" For some reason, I felt a connection with Daniel. Maybe it was because he was friends with Lana, but my gut told me to trust him. I wasn't sure how I felt about getting handed off to a stranger.

"I'm afraid women's fashion is a bit outside my expertise, but I'll help as I can. Really, Erica is exactly who we need. We'll be lucky to have her, especially on such short notice."

"Okay, fine."

"Great! I'll check in with Erica, and one of us will call you tonight." He paused, tenting his fingers over his face for a moment. Then he met my eyes squarely. "Are you seeing anyone?"

Oh, how I wished he'd asked that question last night. The only possible response I could give hurt. "I'm flattered, and you're very much my type, but do you really think it's a good idea for us to get involved right now?"

He blushed and looked away, which made my heart flutter unexpectedly. "Oh, no. No. That's not why I'm asking."

Right. That moment in the parking lot, when I'd thought something passed between us, most have been my imagination. I looked down, praying the floor would swallow me.

"You don't have to sound quite so grossed out."

He cleared his throat. "Let me back up. As soon as we announce your candidacy, Curtis is going to come out swinging. He's going to be looking for ways to discredit you, to bring you down. The obvious first attack will come at your profession. We'll deal with that. He'll also attack your chastity. Are you still seeing the man from the video?"

A rather un-senator-like snort escaped me. "Thankfully, no. We broke up a few months ago. There hasn't been anyone serious since."

"But you do date?" When I hesitated, he continued, "How many dating apps are on your phone?"

"One or two, I think." Six. At least six.

"Delete them. Not just the apps, but take down your profiles, delete all the pictures, and close the accounts. We can't have the media talking about your dating history instead of the issues."

That made sense. I'd be facing enough scrutiny in the coming months. The last thing I wanted was one of my disastrous first dates showing up on the front page of some local paper. "I'll do it as soon as I get home."

"Do it now." He held out one hand. "Or unlock your phone, and I'll do it."

"That's not necessary," I snapped.

Pulling out my phone, I made a big show of unlocking it. Daniel came around the desk to watch as I removed all of my information from each service, closed my accounts, and then deleted the apps. "Should I scrub my phone entirely? Reinstall everything from the backup."

"No, that's okay." He sighed. "Honestly, I wish you were in a long-term relationship. It would help to have someone accompany you to events."

"Can't I bring my mom, like Kevin Spacey and the Oscars?"

"Since Kevin Spacey turned out to be a sexual predator, let's avoid that comparison as much as possible."

Right. My face grew warm. "What about Curtis? Does he need a date for events? I can't imagine that he brings his partner to events if their relationship is a big secret."

Daniel chuckled. "Curtis generally brings his mother. For the same reason as Kevin Spacey, minus the allegations."

"Great. You may have to be my plus one, after all."

"No, you're right. That's not a good idea," he said. "Do you have anyone you could ask? An old friend? I hesitate to suggest a colleague, but maybe a friend of a friend could do it."

"I can bring Lana. She may not be a date, but she'll fit in. And she can help me navigate when things get rocky."

"Wonderful." A slow smile spread across his face. Finally,

he stood and extended one hand. His palm felt warm in mine. "Challenge accepted."

"So, what's the next step?" I asked.

"I'll file the paperwork this first thing Monday morning, then notify the press. I'll spend the rest of the weekend looking for a campaign headquarters and let you know when I find it. Then I'll start calling for volunteers and donors. Normally I don't manage campaigns myself, but we don't have a lot of time here. State law calls for a special election to be held within seventy to eighty days after the announcement, and Tiberius resigned two weeks ago."

Even knowing this was a special election, it hadn't occurred to me that things would happen so fast. My fate would be determined in less than three months.

"You okay? Suddenly you look a little green."

"Yeah, I'm good." The words gave me confidence. Absolutely, I could do this.

# Chapter Six

**Embrace**: This one hurts until you get used to it. Practice your elbow grip, because you're basically just hugging the pole with your elbows while hanging in mid-air.

*- Push and Pole Fitness Tutorials, Vol. 2*

Seconds after I got home, a message popped up on my phone from Lana. *Don't leave me hanging here. How did it go?*

Since texting the entire conversation would take forever, I tapped the button for video chat. A moment later, Lana's smiling heart-shaped face and large oval eyes filled the screen. She wore the glasses I rarely saw, meaning she didn't intend to leave home at all today. Probably putting in another ten hours of work from home at her thankless job. Lana's law firm paid well, but from what I saw, ranked low in employee satisfaction. My friend didn't complain much, but the shadows under her brown eyes spoke volumes. You didn't spend a dozen years as BFFs without knowing when someone was miserable at work.

"That good? You didn't want to message me?" She studied my drawn expression. "Or that bad?"

"Okay, first—you failed to mention that Daniel is utterly delicious."

She wrinkled her nose. "Is he? He's kind of buff for my tastes. And way too tall."

"Too tall? Too muscular? Why are we even friends?" Lana stood at barely five feet in slippers. Even when she wore her highest pole heels and I stood flat on the floor, she barely came up to my shoulder. Of course a guy who stood around six-foot-three wouldn't appeal to her. Meanwhile, tall men were my kryptonite.

"Because we never fight over men?" she asked. "Or possibly because I got everyone to stop calling you The Jolly Blond Giant in high school."

"Valid. Thanks again for that," I said. "Bonus: I stopped bleaching my hair."

"My pleasure. Jerks."

It didn't take long to fill her in on the substance of my meeting with Daniel. When I got to the part about my job being an issue, she rolled her eyes. See? That's what best friends were for. By the time I'd finished, smoke poured out of her ears.

"I can't believe the double standard! There's no shame in being a strong, independent woman. I hope you told him to take his image consultant and shove her where the sun don't shine."

Heh. "I wish. No, I got mad, too, at first."

"Only at first?"

"Well, then I heard a little voice in my ear, saying things like 'dress for the job you want.' Do you know whose voice that was?"

She grumbled and looked down at her nails for a minute before responding. "Oprah?"

"You were right, you know. If I walk around in my workout clothes and show up at the debate dressed for pole, no one is going to vote for me. Yes, it's insulting that people focus on my appearance. But Curtis isn't going door-to-door dressed in sweatpants and a No Boundaries sweatshirt."

"Fair point."

"Winning this election is the only way to show Curtis that he can't tell me how to live."

"So, in order to fight for the right to freedom of expression, you're going to…. stifle your right to free expression?"

"I figured you would appreciate the irony."

"Well, I appreciate how frustrating the world can be some-times," she said. "And I get it. How can I help?"

"There is one thing I couldn't ask Daniel." I'd been too embarrassed, especially after telling him about my degree in political science. Which I did have, but I didn't go to school in New York, so it wasn't quite as useful as if I were running for office in California.

"Yeah?"

"Can you give me a crash course on how the state legisla-ture works? My background is mostly federal. Why are we even having an election in the middle of winter?"

She laughed and sat up straight. "That I can. But first, we should take two minutes and grab some wine."

As soon as we returned to our posts, she gave me an over-view. The New York State legislature was made up of two houses, like Congress (and all the other states, apparently). We had the State Senate and the Assembly. One hundred and fifty people made up the Assembly; the number of Senators could apparently vary (for reasons I asked Lana to save for another time), but there were sixty-three at the moment.

"Or sixty-two, anyway. Since Tiberius resigned."

"Right."

Normally, all the seats in both houses went up for re-election every two years, just like the U.S. House of Representatives. But Lana explained, when someone vacated a seat midterm, the law called for a special election to be held to fill it. The specially elected member would serve until the end of the original term.

"Hold up," I said. "So you're saying, if I win, Curtis could just run again in November and we'd go through this all again?"

She shrugged. "Theoretically, I suppose. Most people who lose an election don't run against the same person twice, but it could happen. If he thinks you're in over your head and won't go for re-election, he might try to get the seat back into Baker hands."

"Then what's the point? I'm running for an office I might lose at the end of the year, anyway."

"Hypothetically? Yes. But the thing with the state senate is —you always have to run again in two years. It's never a guaranteed job for long."

"Why not just leave the spot empty?"

"Because there are some very important votes coming up that the party wants to win. The balance of power is very close, and every vote makes a difference. The Senate isn't going to wait to conduct business until all the seats are filled. Things happen when they happen. And we've got bills on parental leave and minimum wage and health insurance and other really important issues."

"Is that why the party is willing to take a chance on me?"

"I'm sure it is," she said. "You've got a real opportunity to make important changes if you get into the Senate right now. Not to mention, the seat won't stay empty. If you don't run, Curtis gets it, and his vote could be the tie-breaker in the wrong direction."

I thought about Curtis's smug smile, about the look on Helen's face when she showed me the injunction. About the insulting language used in the motion to get the court order against us in the first place.

"You're right. And if he runs against me again, then I will run against that weasel as many times as it takes. I'm going to let the people of Saratoga know that the Morality Police can't stifle freedom of expression. If they're allowed to shut down pole now, what's next?"

"You've got this!"

We raised our glasses at our screens in a toast, and I sent my best friend an air kiss.

"I probably shouldn't drink much more. I can't be hungover if I'm meeting Erica tomorrow."

"Who?"

"The image consultant Daniel wants to hire. If she agrees, we're meeting first thing tomorrow morning.

"Hold up." Her eyes widened. "Erica Wentworth?"

"You know her?" I muttered under my breath, "Maybe you should be the one running."

"I heard that," she said.

"It's just—you know the law. You know how all this works. You hate your job. And apparently, you know all the people involved already."

"I'm a lawyer," she reminded me gently. "It's a relatively small circle in this area. Besides, I don't know Erica well. I just know the name. She's the real deal. She's worked with multiple senator's wives, and she even did a stint in Melania Trump's press office.

"So I've heard. Erica's credentials are fab. But I'm also acutely aware that Melania and I don't exactly have the same ideologies. Why do I even want someone from her staff?"

Lana shook her head. "Oh, no. There are plenty of people in Washington who'll put party ahead of everything, even common sense or morals. But there are also people like Erica, who are more about the ideas, the principles. Her thing is helping people with their public presentation, and she's good at it. She wants people to win or lose based on their message, not how they look when they give it."

Her words reassured me. After all, Lana repeated what Daniel told me. While Daniel might be something of a question mark, Lana was one hundred percent Team Mel. We'd been friends a long time. We'd been through boyfriends and exes (both of us) and lost jobs (mine) and bar exams (hers). She'd guide me through this.

# Chapter Seven

**Teddy Bear:** Another showstopper. This move looks extremely difficult, because you appear to be suspended only by one armpit, but with the back of your hip pressing against the pole, you're totally stable. It always seemed impossible to me, but the first time I tried it, I surprised myself.

*- Push and Pole Fitness Tutorials, Vol. 3*

The next morning, I groaned when my alarm clock went off at the ungodly hour of eight o'clock. One of the nice things about teaching dance was that my work mostly occurred between the hours of four and ten p.m. I'd tried to go to bed early after getting off the phone with Lana, but found myself too jazzed up to sleep. After about twenty minutes of tossing and turning, I'd gone online, researching local history (okay, listening to *Hamilton*), reading up on special election rules, and finally, googling Daniel McCarthy.

I shouldn't have, but I wanted to know more about him.

He'd gone to school with Lana, which I knew, and apparently they both went to school with Erica. There were about a zillion images of him online. The same woman periodically appeared beside him. She was pretty. Tall, thin, with artfully arranged dark hair that must've taken hours, lashes that went on for days, big brown eyes. Creamy skin.

The pictures didn't tell me who she was, but she must have a lot of money to look that good. Still, the mystery woman and Daniel were always within about six inches of each other, often smiling, frequently laughing. It didn't take much to deduce that the two of them were a couple. She looked exactly like the type of woman a man in his position should be with. Ah, well.

So much for my dreams of those freckles. Dating my campaign manager was a terrible idea, anyway.

Still grumbling at the early awakening, I shoved the images from my mind and threw back the covers, shivering in the morning air. Today was going to be busy and stressful. Letting myself go all dreamy-eyed over my campaign manager—or worse, jealous of a total stranger—wasn't going to improve anything. The legislature probably also started its day before noon. If I wanted to do the job I was running for, I'd better get used to dragging myself out of bed early. Might as well start now.

Daniel told me little about Erica other than her bio, so when I opened the door an hour later to find a perfectly coiffed woman about my age, surprise took my breath away. We had the same dark brown hair, the same brown eyes, same peaches 'n cream complexion. She wore a black pin-striped skirt suit with a dove gray blouse and that cost about as much as my mortgage.

Other than our clothes, the primary difference was in our demeanor. She stood like someone shoved a ruler up her butt. Every hair on her head was scraped back into a bun so tight, I wondered how she could blink.

"You must be Melody Martin," she said. "I'm Erica Wentworth."

"Hi, Erica. It's nice to meet you." I extended my hand. "And it's Mel."

She tilted her head a fraction before lifting two fingertips toward me and dropping them the second our skin brushed. Erica was apparently not the type of woman who appreciated a firm handshake. A shame. My grip might be the primary thing I had to offer the good people of New York.

With a start, I realized that she didn't just resemble me: Erica was the woman I'd spent a good portion of last night examining, finding her in picture after picture beside Daniel. She looked a little different without the full-on glam makeup, but it was definitely her.

Humph. He could've mentioned that he was bringing in his girlfriend to make me over. That would've been way less awkward than me figuring it out on my own. And it would've saved me five minutes on the phone gushing to Lana about how hot he was.

"Are you going to invite me in, or just stare?" she asked.

"Oh, sorry. Of course. Please come in." I stepped backward, holding the door open.

Taking in her perfectly-tailored suit made me feel extremely underdressed in my yoga pants and oversized sweatshirt, hair in loose waves around my shoulders, face make-up free. But in my defense, we were supposed to be taking a look in my closet before heading to the mall. How nice did I have to look?

I gestured to my outfit. "I'm sorry. I thought casual would be okay."

"I get that, and normally it would be fine," she said. "But the moment you declare, you're a public figure. Gym clothes are for wearing at the gym only."

"Right. Sorry, I didn't think of that. I'll go change."

"No problem. I'll take a peek around." She moved toward the living room, eyes on my pole. I left her there, racing into my bedroom so I could throw on jeans and a t-shirt. My outfit wasn't nearly as nice as Erica's tailored navy suit, but at least it couldn't be described as "gym clothes." I didn't own any "work clothes," and I wasn't going to wear a cocktail dress to the mall.

When I returned, Erica stood in the far corner, one hand spinning the forty-millimeter chrome pole I installed the day after moving in. "What's this?"

She had to know who I was, what I did for a living. Otherwise, why was she here? But I bit back a sarcastic reply. "That's my fitness pole, for when I work out at home. I also give private lessons here sometimes."

"You're a stripper?"

"No, I'm a certified pole fitness instructor. I happen to know many lovely people who are strippers, but I'm not one of them." "Many" was a bit of an exaggeration, but her tone irked me. My friend Janey used to be a stripper, and people loved her. She was the one who got me into pole.

"Certainly," Erica said. "I guess that's why I'm here. You live in a pretty conservative district, and some people might not recognize the distinction. Especially with Curtis riling them up."

"I can certainly see where ignorant people might ignore the distinction."

"Touché. Unfortunately, we need even ignorant people to vote for you."

Right. She made a good point, although her delivery could use some work. "Isn't this what you're here to help me with? To present a positive public image, to put a good spin on things? To show people who look down on me—or strippers—that there's nothing wrong with teaching pole fitness?"

She shook her head. "No. I'm here to teach you how to behave like a State Senator. Step one, you must dress appropriately at all times, even when exercising. You may not work out naked, especially where other people might see you. You will dress appropriately in public: no yoga pants or tank tops outside of a gym. You'll wear professional attire when you leave the house."

"I don't work out naked. I wear a bra top and booty shorts."

"Okay. Why can't you work out in pants and a shirt that covers your stomach?"

"Because pole works better when you have more skin on the metal."

She started to say something that stopped and tilted her head. "Tell me more."

"It's about friction. For some reason, clothes slide off the pole more easily, unless you have a silicone sleeve, which is really a separate issue. With a sleeve—."

Erica held up one hand. "I don't need a dissertation. Just the summary."

"Right. Skin is what sticks to the pole, not fabric. You need to stick so you don't fall. That's important when learning the moves. I've been doing it long enough that it's not a huge deal, but the lack of clothes still helps with movement. Plus, you get hot."

"Thank you. I'll see what I can do with that. Meanwhile, cover up as much as possible when you leave the house. Business casual clothes at all times."

I opened my mouth to protest that I didn't own any business casual attire, but she kept talking. I'd get some at the mall. My credit card would protest, but my birthday was coming. Mom and Dad usually sent me a nice check, since I couldn't see them much anymore.

"Step two. *This*—" Erica gestured at my pole—"needs to come down. Senators do not have stripper poles in their living rooms."

"It's a fitness pole." I corrected her automatically.

"I don't care what you call it, Ms. Martin. People see it, they think stripper. You need to take it down. If this is going to work, you have to listen to my advice, or there's no point in my being here." Her eyes swept up and down my body. "And trust me, Ms. Martin, if you want to get elected, you're going to need me."

For just a moment, I hated her. I hated stupid Erica Wentworth and her stupid tailored suits and her stupid perfect hair and her perfect nails with every fiber of my being. Erica's look wasn't practical for me. If I grew my nails out as long as hers, I'd stab myself in the boob doing inversions. (It happened.)

But I kept my mouth shut. I'd made a commitment, and darn it, I was going to see this through. Even if a little voice in the back of my mind suggested that the type of people who wouldn't like me the way I already was weren't going to vote for me no matter what. After all, Daniel and I didn't intend to hide my background. There was no point: Curtis knew.

Daniel had explained that we'd get more support being open and honest about my past and my desire to help all people who lived in the district than waiting for Curtis to drop a bombshell at the worst possible moment. Based on what I'd seen at the protest, he would delight in "revealing" me to the world as a sinner, and I didn't need that kind of negative energy.

I also didn't need the negative energy of spending all day arguing with the woman hired to help me get elected. So I bit my tongue and agreed to take the pole down, fingers crossed behind my back.

Besides, the pole was portable. It could go back up whenever I wanted. Like every day when I worked out.

From there, we went into my bedroom. Erica poured through my closet, pulling out one item of clothing after another. I waited while she went through my glittery make-up collection, while she counted my pairs of pole-dancing high heels (thirty-seven).

"Do you own *anything* appropriate?" she finally asked with a sigh.

"Depends on how you define appropriate," I shot back. "I've got tons of clothes that are completely appropriate for teaching fitness classes, especially pole. That's what I do for a living. You ever tried to work out in a business suit?"

"You know that's not what I meant." She glanced at her watch. "Good thing I insisted on meeting early. Get in the car. We're going to the mall."

# Chapter Eight

**Dragon:** Some moves look extremely difficult but are easy. This is one that almost looks effortless when done correctly. However, it takes a lot of strength to hold on. And don't eat right before you try it.

- Push and Pole Fitness Tutorials, Vol. 3

We drove in silence, Erica focusing on the road while I fumed over her comments. Yes, I mostly had workout outfits—because that's what I did for a living! If I'd known a few weeks ago that I was going to need a bunch of fancy clothes, I could've gone shopping.

I wanted to give Erica the benefit of the doubt, but she needed to cut me some slack if this was going to work. Too bad I'd never manage to get her onto the pole. Loosening up enough to have some fun would do her a world of good.

After she parked, instead of heading for one of the department stores, Erica surprised me by entering a locally-owned coffee shop on the outside of the mall. She strode directly to the counter without pausing. "We'll have two cappuccinos for here, please."

Standing a head taller than other people had its benefits. "Actually," I said, "I'll have a large caramel latte with extra whipped cream."

Erica glared back at me. "We're not here for dessert."

I cut her off. "Don't even. I met you, you criticized my home. We're here to shop. I'm willing to wear whatever you tell me, change my hair and my makeup, my entire look. Whatever you want. I'll do whatever you say regarding my image, but you will not mess with my coffee. I want a caramel latte with extra whipped cream."

Behind the counter, the barista chuckled before looking down at the register. Erica's eyes widened before she looked away. If I didn't know better, I'd have sworn she hid a smile. Or even a bit of respect.

Ignoring her, I handed my debit card to the barista. Erica moved over toward the station where people awaited their drinks. I stood about ten feet away, facing out the window.

She didn't speak again until we reached our table. "Making a scene in public does not befit a senator. You have to behave appropriately at all times. At this rate, I don't see how you're going to be ready for the election."

"You've known me for less than three hours."

"And in that time, you've done nothing but challenge me. You're not even trying."

"Not trying?" I dug my fingernails into my palms and counted to five before continuing. "My entire world has flipped upside-down in the past forty-eight hours. I found out my ex was using my house as a sex pad. A video of me falling on my butt went viral. I lost my job. Some total stranger is trying to stop me from teaching. I've never done anything to this guy. I'm not hurting anyone, but he wants to take the one thing I love most in this world. Turns out, the only way to stop him is to run for office myself. Fine. Let's do it. Then I find out that running means changing everything. Okay, whatever. I want to do this. I want to protect my livelihood, protect other people in the same situation. I don't want some rich dude to sweep in and take away everyone's freedom of expression just because he's a total prude. I don't want anyone else to lose their income the way Helen and I did." *Even though Helen screwed me in the end.*

"There! That's it."

I blinked at her. "What?"

"That's the passion and fire you need to win. We have to make people root for you, make them believe in you. Curtis is practically a cardboard cutout of a politician. I'm going to clean up your image, but you've still got to bring the personality. When you're acting like this whole thing is a big inconvenience, it doesn't make anyone believe in you."

Her words touched a nerve. She was right. I'd intentionally put on workout clothes for our first meeting, even though I knew she was fixing my image. I'd fought her on removing the pole, even though it was a stark reminder not only of what I did for a living but also that disastrous video. I'd even ordered the most fattening drink on the menu just to see her reaction.

All because I was mad that Curtis came after me in the first place, and that Daniel wanted me to change my image. Also that she and Daniel were dating, when I wanted him for myself. None of which was Erica's fault, and it wasn't fair to take my frustrations out on her.

"Sorry," I finally said. "I want to do this. Please help me."

She didn't reply at first. She contemplated the inside of her mug for so long, I almost asked her to read my fortune in the grounds.

Finally, she chugged the rest of her cappuccino and stood. I wondered why I'd ever thought she had real emotions. "Come on. We don't have to like each other, but we do have to work together for the next several weeks. We might as well get to it. The sooner I can make you into a politician, the sooner you can start writing me that glowing recommendation."

Grabbing a lid for my latte, I followed her.

"By the way," she said. "The name 'Mel' doesn't fit the image we're going for. From now on, you're Melody."

"Melody Martin? That sounds like a cartoon character."

"And Mel Martin sounds like a crotchety cartoon character," she pointed out. "We need to soften your image. Melody is friendly, approachable. A problem solver."

"No way. Only my mother calls me that." I hated being called Melody. After decades of people pointing out the irony of my mother giving such a name to someone who couldn't carry a tune, I'd be happy to never hear it again. It's not like babies can sing, anyway.

"Great. Then she won't have to make a change." Erica's tone made it clear the subject was closed. She held the door open and gestured with her free hand. "Let's go."

I groaned inwardly, wondering once again what I'd gotten myself into.

Most of my clothes came from the sales section of Athleta or lululemon, the same brands used from Poshmark, or specialty pole stores online. It had been ages since I'd set foot in a department store, and certainly not one this posh. Erica, however, apparently had plenty of experience, as she navigated straight to the section housing rows of evening gowns.

"Oh, this is nice!" I zeroed in on a floor-length, silky green dress with a sweetheart neckline and gorgeous strappy back. The bottom pooled in a slight train.

"You're not a sixteen-year-old girl trying to lose her virginity on prom night. Put that back."

My cheeks burned. The dress looked simple, yet elegant to me. But what to wear was one argument Erica would always win. It was literally her job. Instead of responding, I ducked my head and returned the dress to the rack.

"Politics is a conservative business," she said. "Neutral colors. Blacks, beiges, navy blues."

"You mean, politics is boring," I corrected her. "Why does everyone have to look the same?"

"It's classic," she said, handing me a bunch of dresses that looked more or less identical to me. "Classy. Try these on."

There didn't seem to be any point in trying to pick out my own clothes, so I trailed her to the dressing room. She sat on a bench outside and pulled out her phone. "Show me each one when you're done. And leave your purse out here."

"What?"

"I don't want you in there texting pictures to other people, getting conflicting opinions. No one's thoughts or impressions matter except mine."

"Whatever." It wasn't worth arguing, so I rolled my eyes but handed her my bag before heading into the dressing room to see what she'd come up with.

The first dress was dark beige, with puffed sleeves and buttons halfway up my neck. It looked like something my great-grandmother would've worn if she'd had no taste at all. Erica had to be trolling me. I didn't even bother to try it on before throwing it on the "no" hook.

The second dress was lighter beige, exactly the same shade as my skin tone. Holding it up to my reflection, I realized I'd look naked in it. Erica might know image, but she apparently wasn't a fashion expert. Or, she put it in the stack as some sort of test. It went on the "no" hook as well, unworn.

The third dress was a grey sheath. It wasn't awful as long as I ignored the boxy matching suit jacket. Has anyone worn shoulder pads since the '80s? Still, it was the best one so far, so I slipped it on and looked at myself in the mirror. Then I turned around and burst out laughing.

I stuck my head out the door. "You do not want to see this."

"Show me," Erica said without looking up from her phone.

"It's obscenely short. I'll be flashing my junk all over the party."

Her serious brown eyes met my laughing ones. "Right. That was a test. You passed."

Heh. Yeah, right. Without answering, I pulled my head back in and shut the door. The two remaining dresses in the stack were fine. Boring, but they covered all the important parts and weren't hideous. Assuming I'd be required to attend more than one dressy function in the next couple of weeks, I handed both through the door to Erica and sent her to wait in line while I changed back into my regular clothes.

When I came out, I scanned the line leading to the cash register, but Erica was nowhere in sight. Since I couldn't stand in line without the dresses, I grumbled under my breath while scanning the store.

There. Clear over by Housewares, she was talking to a woman with silvery-white hair, chatting like old friends. I started to call her name but didn't want a reprimand about how senators didn't shout across public spaces. And I couldn't use my phone, because Erica still had my purse.

By the time I reached her side, the other woman had vanished. "Who was that?"

Erica jumped and spun around. "Remind me to teach you not to sneak up on people."

"I didn't sneak. You weren't paying attention, talking to that woman. She a friend of yours?"

"What? No. I've never seen that woman before." She paused. "She was looking for the restroom. Sorry, let's go."

The rest of the shopping trip was more of the same: Erica picking out stuff that covered most of my skin, washed me out, and made me look hideous, while I sifted through for the least objectionable pieces and thought about how to accessorize in a way that might add some personality. At least I had plenty of shoes at home.

Once I gave up arguing, we finished the excursion a little more than an hour later. She made a list of my sizes and let me know that I'd get an email with links to other items to buy online.

"I can't wait," I said. "Can we go now?"

She shook her head. "Of course not. The clothes are only step one. I've made an appointment at a salon. You need a cut, style, and waxing."

My hands went instantly to my hips. "What's wrong with my hair?"

"Nothing, if you're a twenty-two-year-old student. You want people to take you seriously as an adult. That means looking the part. If people think you're playing dress-up, they're less likely to take you seriously."

I refrained from pointing out that a little girl playing dress-up was exactly the way I felt in most of the clothes she'd picked out. One hand went to my hair, which I'd yanked back when we started shopping. A few random locks hung out of the ponytail, tucked behind my ears. It had been ages since I got a cut. And after the past couple of days, a scalp massage would feel amazing.

My credit card protested, but for once, I kept my mouth shut and followed Erica back to the car. After getting in, I couldn't resist making one more comment.

"Did Alexandria Ocasio-Cortez have to put up with all this to run for Congress?"

"I doubt it. She worked for Senator Kennedy's office during college, then for the first Bernie Sanders campaign. I expect she knew how to comport herself before running for office. Everyone harps on her past as a bartender, but she took that job because she needed the money."

"That's why I started teaching pole."

"I believe Ms. Ocasio-Cortez didn't dance in her underwear in public."

"Well, I believe, of all people, AOC would support my right to wear as much or as little as I want."

Erica glanced up sharply. There it was again, the smallest, most begrudging moment of almost respect. She quirked an eyebrow at me, and I knew I'd scored some points.

"By the way, Daniel told me everything about you," she said. "No more pole videos."

Okay, maybe I'd been too hasty about that whole "winning her over" thing. Nothing seemed to be enough for her.

"What are you talking about? The fitness tutorials? That's how I bring in new business to the studio."

"Yes, I realize what they're for. You're done with them. No more posting."

Inside, I seethed, but I gritted my teeth and nodded. No way I would stop making the videos. Eventually, I hoped to be in a position to launch them, especially if I lost this thing and had to take my teaching online because I wasn't allowed to work in this county. She didn't need to know that. I could simply stockpile the files, and upload one a day when this was all over. Preferably from a beach, while holding a drink with an umbrella in it. I suspected I would earn it.

"That's not all," Erica continued. "I've taken a look into this Gary person from that viral video. He's not someone that I want to see you associating with anymore."

A chuckle escaped me. "No worries there. I haven't seen him since that day. You can probably guess why."

She smiled briefly. "Um, yes, I have some thoughts on that matter. Anyway, good. That's it for now then. Any questions?"

One obvious question jumped to mind, but there was no way I could ask her: what on earth had I gotten into?

# Chapter Nine

**Figurehead**: Make sure you're comfortable with a side climb before you try this move. Then wait for the bruises to heal. You'll get into it from a basic climb, but you need a good knee grip.

*- Push and Pole Fitness Tutorials, Vol. 2*

Later that night, Erica dropped me back at my condo with a scathing glance at my pole and a reminder to "remove that thing" before she returned. It took all of my composure to refrain from giving her the finger as she drove away.

Okay, fine, I did it, but behind my back.

Before even making it through the front door, I was scrolling through my contacts to find Daniel's number. He answered on the first ring.

"I'm surprised you made it this long without calling."

"You knew we wouldn't get along?" For some reason, that admission hurt a little bit. Like Daniel didn't believe that I had what it took to make this work. Or he didn't like me, so his girl-friend wouldn't, either.

"Let's just say, Erica is an acquired taste," he said. "At least you weren't texting me from the dressing room at the mall."

"She took my phone," I grumbled. "Just got it back."

Only his deep, rumbling laugh answered me. In other circumstances, it might have been sexy.

"She's a monster," I continued, forgetting for a second I spoke to the monster's boyfriend. Luckily, he didn't get mad. "I don't mind cleaning up my public image, but I can't become a completely different person."

"Of course not. People have to get to know you, to *want* to vote for you, or this will never work. You can't pretend to be a kindergarten teacher and then jump out of a cake at your victory celebration."

I giggled despite myself. "Can someone tell Erica that? She seems to think I'm going to give everything up. She wants me to take my workout pole out of my living room. Said she'll quit if I don't."

"Would it be so terrible to have a living room without a pole in the middle of it?"

"Dancing is my life. It's how I express myself, it's how I blow off steam," I said. "When I can't dance, I get anxious, cranky. I'm more likely to snap at people. More likely to lose my cool, especially in stressful situations. Do you see what I'm getting at?"

"If we take away your dancing shoes, we might as well hand the election to Curtis?"

"Pretty much."

He sighed. "I'll talk to Erica. She's pretty conservative in some ways, but she understands needing an outlet as well as anyone. And I'm sure she'd prefer you pole in private rather than in public if those are our only options."

My spirits rose significantly. Since Erica and Daniel

currently comprised my entire campaign staff, the reminder that he was on my side made me feel a lot better. "I hoped you'd say that. I know that we need her, but I can't give up pole during the most stressful time of my life. I just can't. I'll explode."

"I'll do my best. Anything else?" Daniel asked.

"Yeah, there is one more thing I need from you."

"Your wish is my command." The smile in his voice shone through. "You know, as long as your wish doesn't require too much money from the budget."

"Nope. All I need is you."

"Well, that sounds interesting. I hope you aren't about to ask what I'm wearing."

Picturing Daniel at home, dressed in casual clothes sent a little thrill through me, but I quickly quashed it. He wasn't available to me. Instead, I savored each word, letting him stew on the other end of the line. "One class. You and me. I'm going to show you what pole really is. Be here tomorrow morning at eleven. Wear shorts."

Before he could respond, I hung up.

The next morning dawned bright and sunny, despite being about four degrees. I kept my condo warm, but not warm enough to walk around in my normal pole dancing clothes in the dead of winter. For my lesson with Daniel, I found my least stripper-like ensemble that still allowed free movement. As soon as he arrived, I led him into the living room, giving a lecture about the physics involved in the different movements. Before I could get into the geometry needed to hold various poses, he interrupted me.

"Wait. You were serious?"

"I never joke about pole, Daniel. If you thought I was kidding, why are you in workout clothes?" He wore a soft-looking gray t-shirt that stretched across the muscular biceps I'd mentioned to Lana. His shorts were too long for advanced pole, really, but fine for what we'd be doing. And they gave me a hint of strong legs, just enough to tantalize while I reminded myself to keep my hands to myself.

"It's my day off, and they're comfortable." He shrugged. "I figured we'd have breakfast, chat. Get to know each other."

"And we will. Just not by talking," I said. "If we're going to be working together you need to know me, but you also need to understand my passions. Curtis has an extremely low opinion of pole, and that's why he's come after me. If you're going to work with me, advocate for me, I need you to see the truth."

He nodded. "I get that."

"A lot of thought goes into doing the moves safely. Being successful at pole fitness requires strength, flexibility, and muscle control. It can be incredibly graceful. I suppose it can also be trashy, but anything can be trashy if you want it to be."

To illustrate my point, I sat on the crash mat I'd set up, my legs splayed on either side of the pole. Before Daniel could ask what I was doing, I reached above my head and grasped the pole with both hands, pulling seamlessly upward. My body rose, and I clamped my legs around the pole. His jaw dropped. I repeated the move, climbing up the pole using only upper body strength until I reached the ceiling.

"That's impressive. Mind if I try?"

A lot of men thought climbing the pole was as easy as going up a rope in gym class. In some ways, maybe it was, but this wasn't an easy move. I slid to the ground slowly, then stepped back with a bow. "Not at all. Go for it."

As he sat on the ground, his t-shirt rippled across his back muscles. He grasped the pole just as I had, then yanked. Nothing happened.

"Your forearms should be on the pole," I said helpfully.

Taking his hand in mine, I showed him how to place his arms to get the needed leverage. A jolt of electricity hit me. Static from the pole. If he felt it, too, he didn't react.

Our eyes locked, and I resisted the urge to lick my lips. We had to keep this professional. Stepping back, I gestured at the pole and suggested he try again.

This time, Daniel managed to raise himself about three inches off the ground before dropping back onto his ass with a groan.

"Wow. That's harder than it looks."

"A lot of pole is," I said. "People think it's easy because strippers do it, but that's ridiculous. Pole is a sport. It takes training. That's my point."

Reaching over his head, I grabbed the pole several feet off the ground and climbed again. When I got near the top, I halted, coming to rest in a sitting position.

"Is this all a way of impressing me with how talented you are?" Daniel's voice held a note of awe that thrilled me.

"Maybe a little." I kept my tone light, teasing.

I leaned around the pole, clamping my left armpit around it while gripping with my right hand. My legs rose into the air, pointing away from the pole like a flag flapping in the breeze. Then I pulled my body back in, adjusted my grip, opened my legs into a vee shape, and flipped over so the pole rested between my thighs. My upper body and legs extended outward. I released my bottom hand from the pole and held it out in front of me like a superhero, holding myself aloft with one hand and my thigh muscles.

On the floor, Daniel gazed up at me, eyes as wide as saucers. "How do you do that?"

"How do you get to Carnegie Hall?"

He shook his head with a wry smile. "Practice, practice, practice."

"You got it." I allowed myself to slide down to the ground before rising to my feet. "And now, you're going to learn, too."

He gestured at the pole and swallowed. "I'm going to learn–?"

I laughed. "No, not those moves specifically. Some of that is pretty advanced. We'll start small."

After my demonstration, Daniel turned out to be an eager learner. He had no dance training or experience, but was in good enough shape from the gym that he quickly picked up several basic strength-based moves. After ten minutes, he tugged his t-shirt off and tossed it in the corner. Half an hour later, sweat glistened on his chest, and he begged for a break.

"You know, this may not have been the best way to get me to convince Erica to let you keep the pole," he said as I dropped onto the crash mat beside him. "Not if you're going to use it as a torture device."

I nudged his shoulder playfully, and he pretended to wince. At least, I think he pretended. "Come on. You loved it."

"I did. Surprisingly," he said. "That was a lot of fun."

"Just a workout, right? Nothing sexy or unseemly about it."

"Nothing sexy? I wouldn't go that far." He grinned at me, and a flash in his eyes reminded me of our connection that first night. Maybe I hadn't imagined it. "But your point is well taken. My entire body is going to be sore tomorrow."

Picking up an oversized sweatshirt I'd left in the corner of the room, I gestured for Daniel to follow me into the kitchen. After grabbing his discarded t-shirt, he pulled out one of the bar stools around my island and heaved himself onto it. While he guzzled water, I pulled out cold cuts, bread, cheese, and veggies to make sandwiches.

"You know, as your campaign manager, it's usually up to me to provide lunch."

I shrugged. "I like to cook. This isn't exactly a gourmet meal, but feeding people makes me happy. Much like teaching them."

"Tell me more about yourself," he said.

"I'm an open book. What do you want to know?"

"Everything," he said. "More accurately, everything that

Curtis or the press might dig up during the campaign to try to hurt us. Unpaid debts, bankruptcies, speeding tickets, court cases…Whatever skeletons are in your closet, tell me now. I'll do a full background check at work tomorrow, but I want to hear it from you."

That made sense. We didn't have a lot of time to convince the public that I'd be the best person to represent them in the state legislature. We needed to be prepared. Unfortunately, I'd never thought of myself as terribly interesting. "You want a deeper, darker secret than dancing in my underwear for a living?"

"We're not hiding that."

While I thought about what to share, I returned to slicing tomatoes and onions for our sandwiches. "My parents are in the military, so we moved around a lot when I was a kid. They're still enlisted, living on a base overseas."

"Do you have a good relationship with them?"

"I do. Don't see them as much as I like, but thank goodness for Facetime. My mom is one of my closest friends."

He tapped something on his phone. "Brothers or sisters?"

"None. Also no bankruptcies or judgments. My credit rating is near perfect."

"Great." Another note into the phone. "You deleted those dating apps."

The tiniest lilt in his voice made me wonder if he was asking as Daniel or as my campaign manager. But that was stupid. Campaigning was going to be difficult enough without constantly having to remind myself that my manager was unavailable to me. Since he'd already watched me uninstall everything from my phone, he was probably just trying not to insult me by asking the question.

"Every single one. You know that."

"Good," Daniel said. "Is there anything else I need to know about you?"

*Only that I wish you didn't have a girlfriend,* I didn't say. My eyes roved over him. The shirt he'd put on for lunch clung to his chiseled torso, making it hard to keep my gaze above his neck.

"No, nothing I can think of," I said.

"Sounds like you're ready."

"As I'll ever be."

"Perfect timing. We've got our first public event tomorrow night. A fundraiser. This is your chance to meet the donors."

Excitement filled me at the thought of getting started. "I can't wait."

# Chapter Ten

**Vortex**: This one's probably going to leave some bruises until you get it down. It's cool, I enjoy explaining my armpit bruises at cocktail parties. Call them "pole kisses" and wear them as badges of honor.

*- Push and Pole Fitness Tutorials, Vol. 4*

The next day after work, I decided to go shopping again to pick up a few more "appropriate" outfits, and maybe find a way to look a little less boring at the fundraiser. My initial plan had been to do a workout before I left, but Erica left me with strict instructions *not* to work out before the party. You're apparently not supposed to wash your hair before getting an up-do. Who knew? My hair probably wouldn't look much different if I showered before the party or not, but I needed to look like I was making the effort. Sweaty hair didn't make a good impression on people, and I wanted the donors to like me.

I'd just finished my errands and arrived home when my phone buzzed with a text from Lana. *What time's the fundraiser?*

*You don't have to come*, I replied.

*'Course not. But I want to be there for you.*

*It's not going to be terribly interesting. A lot of donors and party big-wigs sizing me up.*

*That stuff interests me. I interned with the Legislature during law school. Worked on drafting legislation my first year after graduation. I'll be fine.*

A wave of relief hit me. It would be nice to see a friendly face other than my campaign manager. After all, Daniel had to pretend to like me, but he'd probably be bringing his girlfriend. I'd rather let rabid wolves lick peanut butter off my face than spend the evening watching him and Erica together.

The rest of the guests would be people I'd seen on the news or total strangers. I wouldn't have asked Lana to ruin her evening by attending, but after reading her messages again, I realized how badly I needed her there.

*Thanks*, I texted. *You're a lifesaver.*

She sent back a series of emojis that brought a smile to my face. Since I couldn't blow off steam by exercising, I grabbed a cozy mystery I'd been reading and went to run a bath.

The stylist arrived outside my door just as I figured out who the killer was, so I regretfully set the book aside. Erica arrived immediately behind her, and we got to work. Robyn started on my hair while Erica quizzed me on the speech she'd written, prepared me to answer questions that would likely come up, and gave me the background on some of the party's more important donors.

Robyn spun me around. I hadn't worn this much make-up since my last professional competition, a few months ago. I'd placed third, netting a thousand-dollar prize. With luck, this evening would turn out as successful.

Then my gaze moved to my hair, and my jaw dropped. I

couldn't speak. What on earth had Robyn done to me? Tears threatened the corners of my eyes, but I refused to let them fall. Erica met my eyes in the mirror, beaming smugly. My hand itched to slap that smile off her face.

The stylist hadn't given me a new style, as expected. Instead, she slashed the length and shellacked what remained. Instead of my normal free-spirited brown shoulder-length waves, I wore a dark brown helmet that ended at my chin. It made me look about forty years older.

"It's perfect!" Erica said.

Not wanting to insult Robyn's expertise, I fought to choose my words diplomatically. "You don't think it's a little, um, severe?"

"Excuse me," Erica said. "I just need to take this call."

Her phone hadn't rung, betraying the lie. Coward. I wanted to point it out, but the traitor stepped away, leaving me alone with the woman she'd paid very well to destroy my look. I couldn't believe that someone who worked in a salon where the shampoo cost more than most of my bras gave the worst haircut of my entire life.

"No, this is perfect. This style is very popular among female politicians," Robyn said.

"Right. I can see that," I replied. "Out of curiosity, what's the average age of female politicians who wear this haircut?"

She tapped one finger thoughtfully to her lips. "Now that you mention it, I suppose it is a little mature for you. But this is what Erica asked for."

"A little mature? I look like an old schoolmarm!" The words burst out of me so quickly, I couldn't stop them. I held my breath, hoping I didn't offend Robyn.

After a moment, she laughed. Then she leaned forward. "Okay, listen. Erica told me to give you this cut. I worried it wouldn't work, and you're right. It ages you way too much. After she leaves, I'll give you some gel. Wet your hair a little, scrunch the gel in, and let it air dry. You should be okay for the event tonight."

"Are you sure?" Not that I was in the habit of questioning professionals, but the last twenty-four hours had been a great lesson in being careful about who you trust. Even when you're paying them buckets of money.

She nodded. "If not, come by my salon tomorrow without Erica. We'll get you sorted."

Hopefully, getting me sorted would involve extensions or maybe replacing the honey-brown highlights that used to accent my hair. Before I could say anything, the she-devil returned.

"All good? I have to drop by the office, but I'll meet you at the fundraiser."

Wordlessly, I nodded. The less said right now, the better. If only Robyn could give me an entirely new look before I had to leave, but unfortunately, there wasn't time to wash out all the hairspray and start over. I needed to get dressed soon or I'd be late. Not the type of impression to make at my very first public event. Tomorrow would have to be soon enough to fix my hair.

After the two of them left, I pulled out my tablet and opened a video chat with Lana. Sure, I'd see her in less than an hour, but some things couldn't wait.

"Oh, honey, I know imitation is the sincerest form of flattery, but your mom knows you love her. You didn't have to copy her haircut."

My fingers curled into fists. I was going to kill Erica.

"Right? I have trouble believing that turning me into a sixty-year-old former drill sergeant is going to make people want to vote for me."

"It'll be okay," Lana said. "We can fix it. Or…hmmm. I could bring you a hat?"

"I'll see what I can do. Thanks for the confirmation," I said. "But we've got to do something about Erica."

Quickly, I filled her in on everything that happened over the last few days. She listened carefully, nodding once in a while, but not interrupting until I'd finished. Then she leaned back and scrunched up her brow. From experience, I knew she was working through this problem in her head, so I waited for her to speak before saying anything. "What's your end goal here? What outcome do you want?"

"What do you mean?"

"I mean—you're a strong, intelligent, resourceful woman. You love teaching pole. I was surprised to hear you say that you'd decided to run for office instead."

"It's not like I had a choice. Curtis shut me down," I said.

"I still think you'd be amazing at running your own studio."

"Thanks. But Curtis isn't happy with just a temporary injunction. He wants to shut me down for good even if that means changing the laws. Someone has to stop him."

"He's not changing the laws." Lana pressed her lips into a grim line. "Not if I have anything to say about it. I'll use everything I've got to fight him."

"You want to become a lobbyist?"

"If that's what it takes," she said. "Anyway, don't get me wrong—you're doing a wonderful thing, standing up for your rights and free speech. But I'm not sure you're doing it for the right reasons."

"Any reason for standing up for our rights is a good one," I said. "I mean, probably. Listen, Daniel is great. I'm honestly glad you introduced us. It's just been a rough couple of days. Erica's job is to help me seem more responsible, but it's been exhausting. She changed all my clothes, she won't let me teach pole or make videos." I gestured at my head. "She even gave me this ridiculous haircut. Err, no offense to my mom."

She laughed. "It does look ridiculous on you. It's not a cut for a twenty-eight-year-old. Your mom rocks it."

"Fair enough," I said.

Lana bit her lip as if trying to decide whether to say anything else. We'd be seeing each other at the event pretty much as soon as we got off the phone, but I couldn't help wanting to keep her on the line a few minutes longer.

"What is it?"

"What are you talking about?"

"Don't lawyer me, Lana. You're making your 'I have something to say and you're not going to like it' face."

She exhaled slowly. "It's just—Erica was hired to change your *image*. That may be the way people perceive you, but you don't have to change who you *are*. You're vibrant, full of life, innovative. Don't let her take that away from you. You don't have to be a cookie-cutter version of Erica to be good enough to serve in the state senate."

"I know, I know. But they're trying to help."

"They're letting Curtis make the election about you as a person. Change the conversation."

Confusion furrowed my brow. "What do you mean?"

"Make it about the issues. After all, that's why you're running. You're trying to protect free speech and free expression. Freedom of expression includes a lot of things. Like your hair."

Her words brought a smile to my face. As usual, Lana knew exactly what to say to make me feel better. This haircut didn't make or break me as a candidate. I would go along with the image makeover. I would wear the boring clothes Erica picked out, but I would make them my own.

"You're right," I said. "Okay, I can do this. See you soon."

We hung up, and I went into my room to finish getting ready. With my dark brown hair glued to the side of my head, heavy make-up making my eyes look more hazel than brown, the staid dress Erica picked out, and some faux pearls I'd found on clearance that afternoon, I barely recognized the person reflected in the mirror. She looked boring. Older. Worst of all, she had to wear flats because Erica didn't like the idea of me towering over all the male donors.

My upper lip curled involuntarily when my eyes landed on those stupid shoes. Men really wouldn't support a female candidate who was taller than them? Were male egos that frag-ile? Maybe they should come to a pole class. I'd teach them a thing or two about confidence.

# Chapter Eleven

**Corkscrew:** On a static pole, this is a strength hold. On a spinning pole, it's a really cool trick, especially if you spread your legs into a vee. Start by putting your arms in a split grip, making a wide triangle. Then pull your knees into your chest, curving your body around the pole.

*- Push and Pole Fitness Tutorials, Vol. 1*

When I arrived, the fundraiser was in full swing. Erica thankfully didn't feel it was necessary for me to greet guests at the door, and Daniel thought I'd make more of an impression if he announced me once everyone arrived. Then I would give a short speech for maximum impact.

Pausing in the hotel lobby outside the rented conference room, I texted my campaign manager to let him know I'd arrived. Considering the short notice, I'd expected to find maybe four people moving in a sea of empty tables, but well-dressed people packed the room from wall to wall.

Daniel had to be in there somewhere, but he didn't stand out in the sea of suits. Not even his height helped me locate him through the mass of people. I thought I recognized a couple of faces, probably from the posters of party members all over his office. Erica stood in the far corner of the room, with such an unfamiliar expression on her face it took me a minute to recognize it as a smile. She held a glass of champagne in one hand, and she chatted easily with a man in an expensive-looking suit whose face I couldn't see. But none of that is what made me gasp when she caught my attention.

She wore the silky floor-length green dress I'd first pulled off the rack yesterday morning. The one she sneered at me for choosing. My lips pressed into a thin line.

I started across the room, intending to give her a piece of my mind. I didn't make it three steps inside the doors before a hand touched my arm, pulling me to a stop. In my tunnel vision of rage, I hadn't even noticed Daniel coming to meet me.

"Melody! How nice to see you," he said loudly, handing me a glass of champagne. I didn't want it. Trying to hand it back, I mumbled an excuse under my breath, but he moved closer and stood at my elbow. When he spoke again, his voice was low. "I don't know where you're racing off to with murder in your eyes, but you're the belle of the ball and all these people are watching you. Smile. You look lovely. Very professional."

Right. Improving my image probably didn't include screaming at my image consultant in public. I closed my eyes and breathed deeply, counting to five the way I did before practicing a new or difficult move. Then I opened my eyes and forced a smile to my lips.

"Thank you."

"Much better." Daniel's gaze moved up and down, taking in my new look. When he got to my hair, his eyes widened almost imperceptibly. He had a good poker face, but not *that* good.

"That bad?" My hand went instantly to pat my head. I mean, sure, I hated the look, but Mom's hair looked great on her, and people said we resembled each other.

He shook his head. "No, I'm sorry. You look lovely. Just…different."

"Good different, at least? Or different like ready to enter retirement?"

Leaning forward, he kissed my cheek, near enough my lips to send a little thrill through me. A thrill I instantly quelled. This was business only. "You're a knockout in anything, Mel."

"Thanks." I beamed at him, ignoring the butterflies in my stomach. Daniel wasn't available to me, for at least three reasons. "Oh, but call me Melody."

"Sure. Sorry, I thought you preferred Mel, since that's what Lana calls you."

I made a face. "I do, but Erica is insisting that I use my full name to distance the Senate candidate from the dance teacher."

"In my experience, people don't really change, no matter what they call themselves," Daniel said. "But Erica knows best."

Darn it, he was such a great guy. Too bad I couldn't meet someone like him who was single.

"You're a monster by the way," he said. "Every muscle in my body is sore. It hurts to blink. I didn't even know that was possible."

I grinned up at him. The banter helped put me at ease. "You're welcome."

"When I can feel my arms again, I plan to return the favor. We're hitting my gym, and I'm going to make you sweat."

"You're on!" The thought of getting sweaty with him made

my face grow warm. *Purely platonic, Mel.* I surveyed the room while sipping my champagne. Still no sign of Lana.

"This place looks great," I said. "I'm surprised we had room in the budget to set up something so fancy. When you first mentioned having a fundraiser, I thought we'd be hanging out at the local 99 Restaurant."

He shrugged. "My sister's the manager here. She donates the space periodically for events in exchange for the tax write-off."

"Okay. That makes me feel better. At least if I bomb, you didn't waste a ton of money."

"You won't bomb." His confidence put me at ease. After all, Daniel was investing a lot of time and some party money to support me. He wouldn't do it if he didn't believe in me. "You're going to be great tonight. Now laugh like I said something funny."

"A little funny, or hilarious?"

He chuckled. "Funny, but not knee-slapping funny. This isn't the place to let out peals of laughter."

I summoned a mental image of the first time I attempted to spin around the pole by my knees. One leg had slipped off and I went flying across the room, nearly knocking Lana over in the process. Recalling the look on her face, I giggled.

"Much better. Let's go visit the hors d'oeuvres table."

Smart man. I never turned down food, and I hadn't had time to eat since lunch.

My excitement dissipated a bit when we reached the table to survey the offerings. A lot of finger foods, much of it greasy. Some tiny sandwiches, which might be okay if they weren't smothered in mayo. A veggie platter, which looked delicious, but couldn't be considered a full meal. With my metabolism and muscle mass, I needed to eat about twenty-five hundred calories even on non-workout days, which translated to about seventeen of those teeny sandwiches for dinner. People knocked pole, but the daily workouts kept me in better shape than most of them ever dreamed.

Before the next event, I'd have to talk to Daniel about asking the caterers to provide something more substantial. Or eat first. Erica wouldn't approve of me stuffing my face at the buffet table all night when I was supposed to be dazzling people.

Not wanting to show my disappointment, I plastered a smile on my face. "This is amazing! How did you throw everything together on such short notice?"

"I didn't," he said. "The party scheduled this event the day we found out about Tiberius's resignation."

"What if you hadn't found a candidate?"

He shrugged. "We either would have canceled or turned it into a fundraiser for something else. One of the benefits of doing business with family. Luckily, we didn't have to."

"Do you think any of these people will support me?"

"I think it's my job to talk them into it," he said. "Stop fidgeting."

"Sorry." Hoping to see a familiar face, I scanned the crowd again. I didn't see Lana, but my gaze returned to Erica and the guy she was still talking to. The crowd had shifted a bit, and for the first time, I got a view of his face. "Hold on. What's she doing speaking with the enemy? Why is he even here?"

"Erica and I have known Curtis for years," he said. "And I imagine he came to check out the competition."

I didn't ask the big question on my mind, which was *Is it a good idea to hinge my success on someone who is so comfortable with my competition?* Instead, I asked, "Are the three of you friends?"

"We're acquaintances who love a good verbal sparring," he said. "Relax. Erica has been in this business a long time. She has a lot of contacts, and she knows how to work a room. She's also apolitical. She's on money's side, and the party wants this seat badly enough to spend the money."

The idea that she might ditch me if we ran out of money didn't exactly reassure me, but there was no point in arguing about it now. I took another bite of my shrimp cocktail and said nothing. Across the room, Curtis saw us looking and said something to Erica. A moment later, he approached.

"Daniel! How the heck are you? It's been a long time."

"Hello, Curtis." His voice was flat, utterly devoid of emotion.

"Is that any way to greet an old friend? You don't look happy to see me."

"I'm delighted that you spent seventy-five dollars to join us," Daniel said evenly. "You remember Ms. Martin?"

"Yes, of course." Curtis's eyes swept over me in a way that would've been creepy coming from any other guy, but instead made me feel like a kindergartner who wore the wrong costume to the school play. "I almost didn't recognize you with your clothes on."

"Fitness instructors frequently walk around fully clothed, you know," I muttered. "Also, I was wearing a massive coat when we met, you tool."

He wasn't listening. He'd already turned back to Daniel. Not wanting to feel like a third wheel, I made an excuse and went to look for my date. Maybe on the way, I could find Erica and comment on how much I loved her dress. Bitch.

Before I got to Erica, Lana stepped into my path. A genuine smile replaced the forced, now painful look I'd painted on when talking to Curtis.

"Thank goodness you're here. You look right at home."

She glanced down at her tailored navy gown, which definitely did not come off the sales rack at Macy's like mine. It fit her like a glove, and the color made her bronze skin glow. Lana was a brilliant seamstress, and also, she said it was easier to make her own clothes because she was so short. Nothing fit off the rack, anyway. Too bad she didn't have time to make me anything. She'd pulled her shoulder-length black hair back into the sleek chignon that I'd dreamed of wearing this evening. Subtle eyeliner and mascara highlighted her long lashes, but a slash of red lipstick gave her a pop of color. Overall, the effect was absolutely stunning.

"I make an excellent Senator's wingwoman," she said. "I'm here to support you in any way I can."

A server wandered by, the scent of bacon-wrapped shrimp making my stomach growl loudly. I snagged a couple before realizing I had no napkin, no plate, and nowhere to put my used skewers when I finished. Fancy cocktail dresses inexplicably contained no pockets, and my not-remotely-posh purse had been left at home in favor of this impossibly tiny clutch that fit only my keys, my phone, and a lipstick. Lana saved me, offering her empty plate and unused napkin before Daniel approached with a well-dressed older couple.

As we discussed my platform, I examined them carefully. Everyone here looked the same in their expensive suits, enormous diamond earrings (on the women, at least), and perfectly styled hair. How did they look so put together? Tendrils were already escaping my up-do, and I'd barely been here fifteen minutes. If I actually won this thing, I'd have to either hire a full-time stylist to follow me around or shave my head. Erica would love that.

Speaking of the devil, she appeared at Lana's shoulder and apologized for interrupting. With her stood a tall, stocky bald man with a gold earring and a black goatee. He looked like he could bench press a basketball team. The kind of guy who got typecast as a security guard—but probably wasn't flexible enough to touch his toes.

"Melody, I'd like you to meet Jerry Braithwaite," Erica said. "Jerry is a local reporter who has agreed to interview you about the campaign later this week."

"Oh, cool! I can't wait to get some good press." I offered him my hand. "I look forward to working with you."

The older couple turned away, promising a generous donation and wishing us luck. Daniel pulled Erica close with one arm, and she kissed his cheek. "Thanks for coming tonight," Daniel said. "I know it was last minute."

"That dress is gorgeous," Lana added. I wanted to kick her, but she hadn't heard the story yet.

My teeth ground together, but no one noticed. I managed to rearrange my face quickly into a smile. My campaign manager was allowed to have a girlfriend, even if she was pure evil. Even if he were available, this was the worst possible time for me to enter into a relationship with my campaign manager. We needed to keep things professional.

"Oh, this old thing?" Erica smoothed the shimmering fabric over her hips. I couldn't deny that it looked stunning on her, the green cloth vibrant against her skin. But, dammit, that was my dress. I should've just bought it. The sleeveless top and body-hugging cut suited me much more than the frumpy gray sheath she'd talked me into wearing.

"Had it since prom night, right?"

She smirked as her eyes swept me from head-to-toe. "That dress is perfect for you. I love your flats."

My blood boiled when I saw the peep-toed heels poking out the bottom of her gown. I opened my mouth to put her in her place, but Lana spoke first.

"The flats are nice, but Mel's got the most amazing high-heel collection. Towering over everyone else takes a lot of confidence. Her self-possession is one of the reasons we've been BFFs forever." She squeezed my hand and winked. "I'm glad this campaign is going to let everyone see how amazing she is."

Something inside me eased. Everything at the party was foreign, there wasn't any real food, my shoes were stupidly flat,

Daniel wasn't available, Erica sucked all the joy out of my life, but Lana supported me, no matter what.

"Thank you," I mouthed at her behind Erica's back.

Daniel excused himself, and a moment later, a clinking sound filled the room. He stood near a microphone I hadn't noticed being set up, tapping his fork against a champagne glass to command everyone's attention. A moment later, the crowd stood silently, waiting for him to speak.

"Thank you, everyone, for coming tonight," he said. "Thank you to the DNC for setting this up, and huge thanks to our guest of honor, Melody Martin!"

My face grew warm. While of course I knew Daniel planned a big introduction at this event, I hadn't expected to be singled out in front of the crowd while holding a dirty napkin and chugging a glass of champagne. My immediate instinct was to stuff the napkin into my bra, but Lana saved me yet again by taking it.

With Erica's eyes boring holes into me, I forced the corners of my lips upward and moved to stand on the platform beside my campaign manager. He talked about my ties to the community, my love of the Capital District, my passionate spirit, and love of Constitutional freedoms. He also spoke of individualism, bringing in new blood to shake things up rather than sticking with politics as usual.

Around the room, heads started to nod. People seemed to agree with Daniel, to even be happy to see me standing beside them. By the time he finished, I thought I might get a vote or two. He raised his glass. "To Melody!"

"To Melody!" the crowd cheered.

I beamed out at them, feeling excited about my decision for the first time since Daniel questioned my image and professionalism back in his office. Maybe things would be okay. My prepared remarks were short but sweet. Erica may be a pain, but she wrote a decent speech. Okay, fine, a good one. People seemed to be responding to me. A good start.

After I thanked everyone for attending and reminded them to enjoy the appetizers, I rejoined Lana.

"You did great," she said. "We've got people intrigued, excited to learn more about you. That's exactly what you want at one of these events."

"Glad to finally be doing something right," I muttered.

"Shush. You're doing awesome. It's tough to be so far out of your comfort zone."

From here, I couldn't even see my comfort zone. "Thanks. You really do make a terrific Senator's wingwoman."

"And don't you forget it when it's time to pass out staff jobs," she said.

Her response startled me. "You're looking for a new job?"

"I don't know, maybe. Sometimes I think it would be nice to try something new, make more of a difference. But my job is decent for now. I'll be fine." She sipped her champagne as she surveyed the crowd. "That was a great speech."

"Thanks. Erica wrote it," I said. "She's got a way with words."

"She can take time to warm up to new people, but she's good at her job," Lana said. "I know you've had some issues, but I think something's up with her."

My ears perked up. Relationship problems? But not really, because that was more drama I didn't need. "What do you mean?"

She nodded in Erica's direction. "First, those are last season's shoes. They may be expensive, but she's had them at least a year. The Erica I knew wouldn't be caught dead in shoes older than about three months. Also, the price tag for that dress is tucked inside."

"You can tell that?"

"It ruins the line under her arm," Lana said.

Since she was a seamstress and I cared little about nice clothes, I believed her. "Weird, but no big deal."

"Not a big deal, no. But it makes me wonder if she planned to return the dress after she wore it." With a shrug, Lana finished her champagne and set the glass on a nearby tray. "Anyway, congratulations on a successful event. How do you like swimming in the deep end?"

There was no real food at my party, and I was going to pass out if I didn't get some calories soon. I cursed myself for not stopping at a drive-through on the way here, but I couldn't risk showing up with grease stains on my suit. Also, I'd expected there to be food. Everyone who was supposed to be on my side was friendly with my opposition. My campaign manager was dating my image consultant, who just happened to hate me. She looked amazing in the dress she stole from me. She made a much better senator than I ever would, so much that I wondered why she wasn't running herself.

To answer Lana's question, I wasn't sure I liked swimming in the deep end one bit. Was standing up for freedom of expression worth all of this?

# Chapter Twelve

**Boomerang:** When done right, this move feels like you're flying. You'll know when you've got it.

*- Push and Pole Fitness Tutorials, Vol. 1*

Once Daniel introduced me around, the fundraiser turned out to be a lot of fun. Lana got a call from work and had to leave, but by then I'd hit my stride. No one mentioned the viral video, which had been one of my biggest fears for the evening. A lot of people mentioned excitement at the opportunity to vote for someone who wanted to talk about environmental issues and social issues, rather than cutting taxes or stopping immigration.

"All the money in the world doesn't do you any good if we run out of natural resources," I said to one woman. "You can't eat a number in a bank account."

She leaned toward me conspiratorially, eyes dancing. "Don't tell anyone, dear, but I find myself hoping that when we eventually have to abandon Earth for another planet, they'll go back to a barter economy. Imagine all those billionaires who destroyed the planet trying to survive where their money can't buy anything."

The comment made me view my companion in a new light. At first glance, she resembled those billionaires she referenced, with her expensive dress and dripping with gems. But I knew from Daniel that Mrs. Van Houten was a big party donor. She'd inherited loads of money from her parents, but she also donated a lot of it, mostly to environmental charities. Apparently, she also had a bit of a mercenary streak. I didn't quite know what to make of her.

"That would certainly be something," I said, sipping my champagne. "But I do hope to pass laws that will push our eventual defection back a few generations. And I'd love to tax those billionaires enough to bring them down eight or ten tax brackets."

She laughed. "An excellent, very democratic answer. Tell Daniel to expect a donation from my accountant tomorrow."

Connecting with the first big name I spoke with certainly helped me feel more confident in my ability to bring voters around to my way of thinking. We weren't looking for huge corporate fat cats to write checks—indeed, I didn't think most of the big New York companies would appreciate my views on things like corporations paying taxes, cutting CEO salaries, and giving employees a good working environment. But if I could get individuals to support me, we could help narrow the gap between those who blindly voted for Curtis's dad all these years and those who would appreciate having a choice.

Beside me, I nudged Daniel. "Remind me that we need to start making sure people know that Baker Senior is gone and the person currently running is Baker Junior."

He laughed. "We're on it. He's definitely hoping to cash in on the family name. Tiberius's ditching the populous and running away to live in a glorified van down by the river may have tarnished the Baker image a little, but the family's been around forever. Curtis's mom is related to the Schuyler sisters somehow. But people want a fresh face. They want a new voice, and they like having options."

"Ah, there's a campaign slogan. Consider me, Option B."

He chuckled. "You're a breath of fresh air, Melody. You brighten any room. Don't be afraid to let yourself shine."

The words buoyed me through the rest of the evening. Any time I started to feel nervous, I thought back to what Daniel said—and the way he said it. I nibbled on tiny sandwiches, laughed, made small talk, and moved around the room like I owned it. By the time we thanked everyone for coming, I was walking on air.

Then I saw it. Once again, in the far corner of the room, Erica talking to Curtis. Old friends or not, he was still the competition. Had they been chatting this whole time?

It was the end of the night, and my polished image was starting to droop. Mascara smeared under my eyes, and my cheeks were flushed from the heat in the room. Wearing this jacket with the dress may have been appropriate, but I was going to pass out if I didn't get outside soon. My helmet hair remained untouched, but that hardly made me feel any better. In contrast, Erica looked as perfect as the moment she'd arrived. She could've stepped right off the red carpet before dropping by our little soiree. That gorgeous dress—my dress— hugged her curves, somehow making her look taller and more confident.

In my mind's eye, I stormed across the room, ripping her dress off before screaming, "You're supposed to be on my side!"

A terrific plan for maintaining my viral reputation, but not a good way to get votes in a semi-conservative New York district. Also a good way to get fired by my campaign manager on Day 1 of the official campaign. And possibly get hit with an assault charge. Not quite what I needed.

Summoning all of my restraint, I forced myself to go over there and say good-bye to them. It was the right thing to do. Plus, if they were talking about me, maybe I'd hear something.

"Thank you both for coming," I said. "It was lovely to see you."

"Yes, of course," Curtis said. "Excuse me, I need to make a call."

"You did well tonight," Erica said when he was gone. "People seemed to respond to you."

"Thanks." Her praise made me feel generous, even though I was still pissed about the dress. "Your speech was killer."

"That's why they pay me the big bucks. I'm sure you didn't think it was my personality."

I snorted. At least she understood how she could come across. That went a long way toward raising my opinion of her. Well, that and seeing the results of her hard work. This event had been a smashing success. Like it or not, she deserved a lot of credit.

When Daniel arrived with my coat, I almost swooned with relief at realizing that I'd made it through the evening without embarrassing any of us. I thanked him profusely for his help and turned to leave.

"Hold on a minute," he said. "I'll walk you out."

Despite my desire to get away from Erica as soon as possible, I waited. To my surprise, he nodded a curt good-bye at her before going to speak briefly to someone I didn't recognize. A moment later, he reappeared at my side. "Shall we?"

If my manager noticed the drastic change in my mood from earlier in the evening, he didn't comment. Snow had started to fall, so we focused on navigating the sidewalk. As the flakes drifted around us, my mind drifted to all these people who'd come out to see me. I wondered what they would think of me, of my job, if they knew. How I would get them to vote for me. But no matter how I tried to distract myself, I remained very aware that Daniel was walking beside me, his arm close enough to brush against mine as he guided me through the slushy parking lot.

Walking me to the car seemed beyond campaign manager duties. Maybe the two of us were becoming friends.

Finally, the question that had been burning in my throat leaped out of me, interrupting something Daniel was saying about preparation. But in my current state, I couldn't even pay attention to him. "Why aren't the two of you leaving together?"

"What? Who?"

"Erica!"

A bark of laughter escaped him. "Why would I go home with Erica?"

His expression brought a wave of heat to my face. I hadn't expected to need to explain this one. "Um… I googled you, and I thought… you two…Aren't you a couple?"

"Oh! Well, that explains a lot," he said, almost to himself. "No. I've known Erica since college. During my freshman year, she dated my roommate. If I recall correctly, Frank dumped her after a few months because she was saving herself for marriage."

"Classy guy."

"Last I heard, he'd made a series of YouTube videos where he burps various national anthems."

"Please tell me you're joking."

"I wish. He's got over a million subscribers."

"Wow. That's…depressing, actually." I contemplated that for a moment, before Daniel's earlier words sank in. "What does that explain?"

He stopped in his tracks, looking puzzled. "What does what explain?"

"When I said I thought you and Erica were a couple… what does that explain?"

"Nothing." He cleared his throat, looking over my head. "Forget I said anything."

We were almost to my car, but I didn't want this conversation to end. I stopped and turned to face him. He stood closer than I realized. "No. Daniel, what does that explain? What are you talking about?"

He sighed and glanced around before meeting my gaze. "When we first met, in the parking lot—there was a definite spark. I liked you. Of course I did. You're pretty. You're self-possessed and able to laugh at yourself."

Each word he said made me feel lighter. "I liked you, too."

"And until you showed up in my office as my candidate, I hoped you were going to call. I wanted to see you again."

"Oh." My smile fell. As amazing as it was to hear that he'd liked me, too, our timing sucked. "I wanted to call you, but this seemed like such a bad time to start a relationship… and then in your office, well, it seemed like an even worse idea."

"Especially because I told you not to date."

"Well, yeah." I sighed. "Anyway, then I saw the pictures, and I assumed you were with Erica, so it didn't matter that you're smart and good-looking and easy to talk to—"

He put one finger to my lips. "Erica and I are old friends. You should've checked the dates on those pictures. She used to accompany me to events sometimes, but that was years ago."

I blinked at him several times. "So you're exes?"

"No. We worked together on a campaign for Marlowe Wright, back before she moved to D.C. We attended some events together as friends. She was married at the time. Moved back to Albany after her divorce."

"I feel like I shouldn't admit how relieved I am to hear that."

He swept an errant eyelash off my cheek, hand lingering

on my cheek for a heartbeat too long. I couldn't breathe. "I know exactly how you feel."

My heart pounded.

Leaning forward, Daniel brought his lips close to my ear. I shivered in a way that had nothing to do with the cold. "If we weren't in public, I'd be kissing you right now."

"Erica would kill us," I said. "But it would be worth it."

Smiling, he stepped back. He held out one hand, and when I took it, he lifted my fingers to his lips. Eyes never leaving mine, he moved slowly, an inch at a time. The anticipation thickened the air around us, and still I couldn't move. Couldn't say a word that might break the spell. When he finally kissed the back of my hand, a breathy sound escaped me. Half-moan, half-sigh. I'd never felt such an intense passion for someone I wasn't already dating.

Then he straightened and released me. "I'll see you at the office tomorrow?"

My mouth was so dry, I couldn't speak. Instead, I simply nodded.

After getting into the car, I sat there, watching him walk away. I caressed the spot where he'd kissed my hand before holding it against my lips.

And none of it could mean anything. The timing was terrible. Daniel was my campaign manager. My opponent was desperate to prove I was a woman of loose morals, and my image consultant would throw a fit. Even if I got elected, it wouldn't be appropriate. People would talk.

Who knew the most difficult part about running for office would be not losing my heart?

# Chapter Thirteen

**Yogini:** Practice this one from the floor until you're sure your armpit can hold your weight. You may also want to put down a crash mat, because you don't want to land hard on your knees. This is the bow pose in yoga, except you're hanging in mid-air.

*- Push and Pole Fitness Tutorials, Vol. 3*

Since I no longer had a job to go to, the next morning I showed up bright and early at campaign headquarters to find out how I could help. If I didn't stay busy over the next two months, I'd start climbing the walls out of sheer frustration. There must be something to do that was more productive than smiling prettily at the cameras, giving soundbites to the media, and shopping for ugly, uncomfortable clothes.

Or lying in bed, staring at the ceiling, and thinking about that moment with Daniel after the fundraiser. It had been a mistake to admit having feelings for him. We needed to keep a professional distance if this thing was ever going to work. I knew it, and he knew it.

According to my phone, the address Daniel had texted me was an ammo supply store that went out of business a few months earlier. A sign remained in the window, offering buy one get one free on certain…brands of bullets? To be honest, I had no idea what the ad was for.

I found him inside the room, sweeping debris off the floor. He wore a suit similar to the one from the night we met. I'd never thought of myself as someone who went for men in suits, but that light blue shirt and gray-striped tie made my stomach do flip flops.

"Interesting choice of office," I said, handing him a latte. Then I turned and removed the sign from the window. "I see we're out of business already."

"Oops. Thanks. 'Choice' isn't the word I would use," he said. "It's local, it was available on short notice, and I know the guy who owns the building, so we got a deal."

I raised an eyebrow at him. "You friends with a lot of gun people?"

"No. His ex-wife managed the rentals before they split. Heavy emphasis on the *ex*." He sipped from his cup, then turned into the room. "Let me take you on a tour."

The prior tenant never removed their glass display counters, so Daniel had shoved them against the far wall before I arrived. For now, they were covered with stacks of paper. In the middle of the room, two desks with giant monitors and phones sat facing the door, waiting to greet anyone who should happen to stumble onto the premises. Hopefully unarmed.

When we finished, Daniel turned to me and cleared his throat. "About last night…"

I shook my head, not wanting to hear him dash my hopes all over again. "I know what you're going to say. It's not a good idea. Let's just put it behind us and move on, okay? Focus on the election."

"Yeah." He nodded, then took a long drink from his coffee. "Great. I'm, uh, glad you agree."

"Awesome!" The word sounded as forced as it felt. "Should we get to work?"

Since I was at the moment the only volunteer, there was no time to waste. First, we took the time to set up a couple more desks for when we got additional workers. Cheap, but usable. They say if you really want to know someone, you should build furniture with them. Instead of wasting time arguing, Daniel simply pointed me at the desk on the right while he started on the one on the left. He probably didn't intend for it to be a race, but, well…I won.

Sure, mine wobbled a little when I set it in place, but the ground looked pretty uneven here. Daniel's creation stood firmly against the tile floor, but he had three screws left over. Mentally, I made a note of which desk he'd made so I would never, ever sit at it. And maybe check it over after he went to lunch. Those screws could be important.

"Hold on a sec." He bent down and crawled under my desk.

I tried not to admire the view. Never had a pair of charcoal-gray trousers looked so appealing. "Everything okay?"

"Absolutely." He backed out and grasped the edges of the desk. He wriggled it back and forth. It remained firm. "There you go."

"Did you just use the extra screws from your desk to level mine?"

The tips of his ears turned red. "Actually, I used a couple of loose bullets I found in one of the display cases."

I laughed. "I hope this doesn't mean I have to support the gun lobby now that they are literally supporting me."

Finally, we were ready to get to work on the actual

campaigning. I'd never done anything like this before, but how hard could it be? Step one: phone calls.

"It's pretty easy," Daniel said. "Give your name, tell them you're calling from the Melody Martin campaign. If you're not comfortable letting them know you're the candidate, give a fake first name. Ask if they've heard about the special election. Here are your scripts for virtually anything they might say. Any questions?"

I eyed the stack of paper he held out dubiously. "Is there an electronic version?"

"Yes." He pointed at the computer on the nearest desk. "Everything your heart could desire. With hyperlinks. Go ahead and read through it. Let me know if you have questions or need anything. Start making calls as soon as you're ready."

"I'll be fine," I said. "I talk to people for a living, remember? It's all about how you say it, not what you say."

"You sound like JFK. With that kind of confidence, you'll do great. Good luck."

Unfortunately, my confidence petered out quickly. The first three people I managed to get on the phone hung up on me. The fourth asked me if I'd found Jesus, and I couldn't find the appropriate response in any of my scripts.

"Jesus? Did you try looking behind the couch?" That probably wasn't the answer she expected. When I realized what I'd said, I hung up, face burning.

From the desk behind me, Daniel unsuccessfully tried to hide a smile. "Did you just…?"

"Yeah. She asked; I panicked."

Dread filled me at the thought of getting fired from my own campaign on the first day, but a peal of laughter filled the room. "Remind me to make a few more scripts for you."

Before I could respond, he stood, grabbing a stack of fliers from the desk. "I'm headed to the local college to find some interns. You shouldn't have to spend your time making these calls when there are more important things you could be doing."

I also shouldn't be making calls when I had no experience, no idea what I was doing, and no filter. But I wanted to feel useful. "I don't mind making the calls."

"I appreciate that, but we need support. Once we have interns, you and I can focus on the real campaigning: hammering out your platform, drafting press releases, preparing you for interviews, wooing the party bigwigs. I'll be back in an hour with lunch. Text me your order?"

"No problem," I said. "Meanwhile, I'll try to stick to the scripts."

Eleven calls later, I found a voter who seemed interested in talking about the special election. She asked one question after another about my positions on child support, abortion, immigration, taxes, everything. As I spoke, she responded enthusiastically. I read one talking point after another from my sheet.

"That all sounds lovely, dear," the woman said. "I'll be sure to register before November."

She wasn't even registered? Why was she on my list? The election was in nine weeks. "This is a special election ma'am, meaning that it's being held separate from the general presidential election."

"Oh, yes, I know. Every election is special."

"What I'm trying to say is to cast your vote for Ms. Martin, it's necessary to register to vote as soon as possible. The election is coming up in two months."

The woman laughed. "You can't fool me. I know Election Day is the first Tuesday in November!"

The phone went dead. Yikes.

With a groan, I glanced at the clock. It was only nine-thirty, and it felt like I'd been here about ten hours. At this rate, I'd never make it through the day. I helped the time pass by making a list of ways to break up the calls with exercise.

- *No answer? 10 squats.*
- *Hang-up? 10 push-ups.*
- *Profanity from a potential voter? 10 crunches.*
- *Someone who admits being unregistered? 5 burpees.*
- *A registered voter who is actually interested and promises to vote? SIGN UP FOR AN IRONMAN, BECAUSE THAT'S NOT GOING TO HAPPEN.*

With a sigh, I pushed the list away and kept dialing. An hour later, much of my nervous frustration had been burned away by squats and push-ups, but I'd yet to connect with a single voter.

What a mess this all turned into. All I had wanted was to find a nice, open space where I could install some poles and work with my students. Helen gave me that. But now, after one run-in with the wrong person, I was unemployed, running for local office to ensure that no one could ever shut me down again.

With a sigh, I laid my head on the desk. Lana had said that Curtis was never likely to manage to prohibit pole statewide, even if he won. She also said he could convince the legislature to pass a law that would allow each city or county to decide on their own whether to allow certain "obscene conduct." That was one of those funny legal phrases that wasn't well-defined, apparently, which meant every locality could decide on their own what to allow, and we were in a conservative area.

She thought that kind of bill might have more of a chance because his side would have a majority if he won. Considering the way politics had recently skewed toward party over policies, all he'd have to do is call his cronies on the local city council, and game over. I'd be left either moving out of state or coming up with a new source of income. Going out of state meant starting over again, in a new place where I didn't know anyone. I could do it, of course, but it hurt to have to pick up when I'd finally started to feel like I belonged somewhere.

These thoughts were going to make me spiral, which I couldn't afford. To distract myself until Daniel returned, I went back to my phone list, promising myself that after every ten frustrating calls, I could do ten leg raises per call. It was the only way to make the work bearable.

Twenty minutes later, I laid on the floor, head against one of the support beams in the middle of the floor. Hands wrapped around the beam, I lifted my legs slowly off the floor, bending in half and touching the floor behind my head. One beat at a time, I lowered them, hovering a couple of inches above the floor before starting again.

Halfway through my third set, I paused to catch my breath, resting my legs on either side of the beam. That's when I heard the lock on the front door clack open.

Someone gasped.

Then I heard Daniel's voice. He sounded almost as if he was choking. "Melody? What are you doing?"

He'd returned earlier than expected, with the promised interns in tow. A girl with long blonde pigtails and glasses watched me with an inscrutable expression, while an Asian guy stared, mouth hanging open. Behind them both, Daniel pressed his lips together, shoulders shaking. He turned away with the effort of controlling his laughter.

"Melody, these are our new interns, Jade and Seth. Guys, meet Melody. She's our candidate."

# Chapter Fourteen

**Cobra:** Floor work isn't my favorite, but sometimes you need to catch your breath between all the gravity-defying tricks. This is similar to the Cobra yoga pose, except you've got a pole between your legs and you'll arch your back to grip the pole above your head.

*- Push and Pole Fitness Tutorials, Vol. 1*

At the last minute, Daniel arranged for me to attend a fundraiser for the local fireman's association on Tuesday night. He apologized repeatedly for the lack of notice when he told me, but my traitorous heart sped up at the thought of getting to spend another evening with him so soon.

I texted Lana to see if she was free on such short notice. Even if she weren't, she'd find a way to join me. That's what best friends did. Knowing how I felt about Daniel, she'd serve as my human buffer.

After Lana agreed to meet me at the event, I put on a

brand-new, knee-length navy wrap dress and attacked my terrible hair. There hadn't been time to get the extensions yet with all the shopping and studying and making pointless phone calls, but I swore to call the stylist first thing tomorrow. Meanwhile, I spent about twenty minutes watching short hair tutorials on YouTube before I came up with something workable.

Once my mane was tamed, I added some subtle make-up and eschewed my preferred six-inch silver stilettos for some boring navy three-inch heels. Erica would approve. Then, I pasted on a smile and headed to the event, the picture of a demure politician.

To my surprise, Lana and I found ourselves seated at a table with the Assistant Attorney General, three members of the state legislature, and Curtis. No one needed to introduce me to the woman sitting beside him. Even if Daniel hadn't told me that my rival tended to bring his mother to events as his date, there could be no mistaking her. Curtis's features fit his face so perfectly, seeing them on the face of a sixty-year-old woman tripped me out. Mother and son shared the same deep-set blue eyes, the same pointed chin, the same charismatic smile, as if Curtis's father contributed not a drop to his genetic makeup.

Across the table, Curtis ignored me and Lana while he vied for the governor's attention. While we ate, the AAG presided over the table, making small talk and artfully drawing everyone into the conversation. Now, she was the perfect politician. I tried to picture myself holding court at a table like this in the future, including everyone, making small talk. No colorful language or controversial opinions. No one made any waves, despite the fact that according to Daniel, the AAG didn't share opinions with Curtis or at least one of the legislators at our table.

As the conversation unfolded around me, I smiled and nodded pleasantly, chuckled when appropriate, and contributed when possible. Lana did a great job making friends on my behalf, and I eventually relaxed. Between dinner and dessert, she excused herself to visit the ladies' room.

The value of circling the room wasn't lost on me, not at all. But Daniel had gotten delayed, and I preferred to have him or Lana by my side before I started introducing myself as a candidate to strangers in a bipartisan room.

While I waited for one of them to appear, Curtis's mother turned to her son. Now that I took a closer look, Mrs. Baker seemed familiar, but I couldn't figure out where I'd seen her before. Not that it mattered. It was probably just the strong family resemblance. "Dear, aren't you going to introduce me to this lovely young woman?"

A look of confusion crossed his face. "Who? Ms. Martin?"

"It's nice to meet you. How do you know my son?" She smiled at me. The way she looked between us suggested she was hoping to do a little matchmaking, which meant she didn't have the first idea who I was. Or who her son was, for that matter.

"It's lovely to meet you, too, Mrs. Baker," I said.

"You look familiar." If I'd hoped ignoring her question would allow me to change the subject, I was wrong. "Have you and my son known each other long?"

"No, we met last week."

Curtis cleared his throat. "Mom, Melody works at Dance 4 U. She's the woman from that video."

Never in my life had I seen someone go from friendly to cold so fast. I could've sworn a rush of chilly wind came out of Mrs. Baker's chest. "Oh. So have you been worshipping the devil long, then?"

A bark of laughter escaped me. "I don't worship the devil. I just like to dance."

"Dancing is how the devil works his way in. You can't be too careful." She picked up her napkin and fanned herself.

"Luckily, my boy is going to join the state legislature and put a stop to all that nonsense. No more sin businesses in our town."

Being polite was getting me nowhere. "Not if I have anything to say about it."

"I beg your pardon?"

"I'm also running in the special election."

"Curty? What's she talking about, dear?"

"Curty?" I mouthed at him, carefully keeping my grin from getting too wide.

He tugged at the collar of his shirt, at least having the sense to look embarrassed at letting the conversation get this far. "Melody is my opponent, Mother." To me, he said, "You're still running?"

His indifference made my blood boil. As if the fact of my name on the ballot were completely inconsequential. "They haven't held the election yet, have they?"

Curtis arched an eyebrow, which made me want to smack him because I couldn't do it. "I'd hoped maybe you'd realized that the venture is pointless and decided to save us both some time and money."

"Sorry if having to actually campaign is a hardship," I said. "But I'm not going anywhere. I need to make sure free expression stays safe for everyone, not just the rich and the privileged."

"People with money are in a better position to evaluate the needs of the masses because they aren't preoccupied with scrounging up food and shelter."

What a load of garbage. "Maybe it's better to leave the decision-making up to those most affected by the policies. We weren't all born with a silver spoon up our butts."

Mrs. Baker gasped at my language. I ignored her.

"Speaking of silver spoons, it looks like they're serving dessert. Everyone should be returning to the table," Curtis said.

"Does the Assistant Attorney General know what you do for a living?" Mrs. Baker said.

I blinked at her several times. "Excuse me?"

"Does she know that you dance naked in front of strangers? I should think that's not the type of person she'd want to dine with."

"That's not what I do."

"That's not how I understand it," she said. "I thought you were running for the right to dance naked."

I glanced at Curtis, but there was no help coming from that corner.

"It's about free expression. The First Amendment is a bit more than dancing," I said. "With or without clothes Which, by the way, I wear. I don't get why you all think I'm naked all the time."

Mrs. Baker ignored half of what I said. "The First Amendment is about the Bible. And protecting people like me from having to associate with someone like you."

"People like me? Oh, I get it. You're one of those people who cherry-picks scripture, right? Gays are bad, but cotton-silk blends are fine? You pretend not to think less of your gay friends and family while actively fighting against their rights?"

"You must have me confused with someone else," she said. "We fight the good fight. I don't associate with any sinners."

I glanced at Curtis, whose face had gone white. He was clearly terrified of his mother finding out about him. Instantly, the fight went out of me. Instead of responding, I pushed my chair back and rose to my feet. "Excuse me. I didn't come here to be abused. I have campaigning to do."

My blood boiled. The rest of the room faded away, and for a moment, I didn't care about the election, the other people in this room, the studio, any of it. Meditation. In and out. Slow breathing.

To my great relief, I spotted Daniel across the room, talking to Lana near the entrance. Exactly the people I needed to see right then. Keeping my eyes on them, I inhaled and exhaled until I felt like myself again.

When I approached, Lana took one look at my face and handed me a glass of champagne from a nearby tray. "What happened?"

"Let's just say I discovered first-hand where Curtis got his horrific views."

"Ah, I see that Mrs. Baker is here," Daniel said. "I'm sorry."

In my tiny purse, my phone beeped. I should leave it. All the people I needed to talk to were in this room, but I couldn't resist. My DNA required me to check my phone when it went off.

I had a text from an unknown number. The message was short and to the point.

*Thank you.*

That was all it said. I had no idea who sent it.

My eyes landed on Curtis, still sitting beside his mother. He watched me intently before his eyes slid to his phone, lying on the table. Suddenly, I knew who sent the text, even if I didn't know where he would've gotten my number. He put on airs, a great show of confidence, but inside, I saw someone who was terrified of disappointing his mother. Of living a life that she clearly wouldn't approve of. He saw firsthand the way she talked to me in public. What might she say to him in private?

Instead of responding, I gave the briefest of nods. I didn't like him, I didn't like his views, but that secret would forever be safe with me.

"Do you know Curtis's father?" I asked Daniel.

"Only by reputation," he said. "Why?"

"Just wondering if he is as rigid as his wife. Or if he was, before his 'epiphany.'"

"I believe so, yes." Our eyes met, and a wealth of information passed between us in a single look. Suddenly, I understood my opponent far better than I ever wanted to. Poor guy.

But understanding Curtis—and even empathizing with his plight—didn't mean I agreed with his actions or his politics. I still couldn't let him take away my livelihood. I took a swig of champagne and put my hand on Daniel's elbow. "Come on. Let me wow these people."

# Chapter Fifteen

**Twisted Star:** This move is actually a great stretch for your shoulder. I like to do it from the ground at the end of a long workout. But it IS more impressive if you can swing into it from a climb, especially on the spinning pole.

*- Push and Pole Fitness Tutorials, Vol. 1*

The days blurred together: fundraising event, press event, looking pretty, waving, making small talk. Endless phone calls. Teeth bleaching, waxing, although I drew the line at tanning in the middle of winter, and I flat-out refused to discuss Botox. Nothing Erica possibly said could change my mind about that one. I wasn't even thirty; I didn't care if I had laugh lines.

More shopping, buying more overpriced junk no one needed just so I looked the part. When I mentioned using an online service to rent the clothes I'd be wearing for the next few weeks, Erica put one hand over her chest and closed her eyes for so long, I wondered if I'd given her a heart attack.

Her response was direct and to the point. "No."

"But—"

"No."

Part of me wanted to argue to see if it was possible to piss her off, but upsetting Erica only hurt me in the long run. After my session with Daniel, she'd arrived at my door with an Allen wrench to remove the pole from my living room.

I'd called him the moment she arrived, but it turned out, since they weren't dating like I thought, he had less sway than I'd imagined over her.

"I'm so sorry, Mel," he'd said. "I'd told her to leave it, but she said you'd get it back once the campaign is over."

"It's two against one, though," I'd pointed out.

"This isn't a democracy," Erica called from where she'd been struggling with the pole. "You could help me with this."

In response, I'd simply snorted and returned to the phone. "Daniel, please?"

"I know it sucks, but she's not willing to discuss this one," he'd said. "And the thing is, we still need her. You're doing great, but we've got weeks left and a lot of public appearances."

The annoying thing was, he'd been right. We did need Erica. People responded to the speeches she'd written for me. They looked at me approvingly at events and interviews. For the first time since this all started, I felt like a political candidate. She also handled press inquiries, and she shone in that capacity. Even if she didn't excel at her job, there was no time to replace her. But she was the best.

"You owe me," I'd finally said to Daniel as I watched Erica walk out the door with my most prized possession. I hoped she would drop it on her foot, but no such luck.

Sure, I could buy another one, but battling Erica took a lot of energy out of me. We needed to get along if this was going to work. So I bit my tongue, gave up my workouts for the time being, and bought more clothes that made me look like a senator. If I lost the election, I'd donate everything to the area women's shelters. Actually, I was half-tempted to do that if I won, too, but I wouldn't. AOC dressed professionally to go to work in the House of Representatives, and so would I.

She had become my idol. We agreed on most policy issues. She was so well-spoken and intelligent, I wished she would run for governor or the Senate just so I could vote for her. Every day I logged into Twitter, Instagram, and Facebook to see what she had said. Every day I sent her messages, hoping that one of her staffers would see my calls for assistance and say something positive about me and my campaign. No response yet, but nevertheless, I persisted. My official accounts emulated hers, from a similar-looking profile picture to the way I spoke.

Now that my wardrobe was complete and I'd made it through a couple of public appearances without completely embarrassing my campaign, I felt better about my chances of winning. Erica still had plenty of ideas for improvement, though.

"We need to work on the way you talk," she said one snowy afternoon out of the blue.

I rolled my eyes. Sure, being cooped up in the office was boring, but was it that boring? "Really? Should I affect a British accent? 'The rain in Spain falls mainly in the plain.'"

"This isn't *My Fair Lady*. We're not going to fall in love and live happily ever after."

"Amen to that, Henry Higgins."

She glared at me impatiently. "If you're not going to take this seriously, what am I even doing here?"

I resisted the urge to throw down my pen in a huff. Instead, I took a deep breath and counted to five. Ten. Twenty. "I am taking this seriously, I promise. It's my livelihood at stake. I want to win this thing. I just don't know that changing my diction is the answer. Don't voters like someone who gives it to them straight? Talks like one of them?"

"Only if you're old, rich, white, and male."

"Is one out of four good enough?" This I asked sheepishly since we both knew the answer. "Sorry. Okay, let's start over. I've got an hour free now, then I'm supposed to have lunch with Daniel."

"I'm glad you mentioned that," she said. "I believe he spoke with you about dating when you signed up. I don't have to tell you how inappropriate it would be for you to date your campaign manager."

Uh-oh. My Spidey senses told me to tread carefully. Somehow, Erica had dialed into the chemistry between me and Daniel, and she didn't like it at all. Not that I blamed her. I'd been fighting our attraction from the beginning for all the reasons she was now preparing to list.

For once, I forced myself to resist going on the offensive. "I appreciate your concern, but Daniel and I aren't dating. It's a business lunch."

She snorted. "There are eyes and ears everywhere."

Daniel was smart, funny, interesting, supportive, and kind. Not to mention smoking hot. If Erica was going to penalize me for dating him, at the very least, I should be allowed to actually date him.

"Great. Tell your eyes and ears nothing is going on. Which they'll see for themselves if you want to have someone follow me to lunch. Just don't sit with us."

She stared at me for a long moment. I gazed back defiantly, refusing to break eye contact. I'd compromised on virtually everything so far. Okay, well, I'd changed my hair back, so I looked my age. On everything else, I caved. Not this time. Not when I wasn't doing anything wrong.

Finally, she huffed and looked away. "Good. It's much better not to be casually dating while campaigning."

"Oh really? And is Curtis's private life being watched and evaluated until the results are in?" From what Daniel had told me, Curtis had some experience keeping the public from finding out about his relationships. Maybe he could give us some tips.

"This isn't about him," she insisted. "This is about you and the image you portray to the public."

"As far as the public is concerned, I'm a nun," I said dryly. "A nun who poles."

"Keep it that way. Because if I find out you're lying to me, I'll leave you without a backward glance."

"The door's over there." To emphasize my point, I threw my arm out in that direction.

She sighed. "Fine. Let's go back to diction. You're a straight shooter, Melody. A lot of people like that. Just not in a woman who's running for office. And no swearing."

Since I'd won the last battle, this time I gave her my full attention. Not swearing was easy. Well, doable. Avoiding words like "crap" required some conscious effort, but I'd manage. If being more reserved was what it took to get votes, more reserved I could be.

We seemed to have reached a truce by the end of the day. Erica announced that she had an errand to run and that she'd be back later. More likely, she was as sick of me as I of her, but I let her go. We both needed some time apart.

I sent Seth and Jade home early. They'd been working hard, and everyone could use a break. Daniel went for a walk to clear his head before rewriting a speech he was preparing for the local public access station. I badly wanted to go home, but Seth had emailed me a ton of stuff to read through, touching on virtually every vote the legislature had made or was expected to make before the end of the session, and I needed to review it. Sure, I could read at home, but there, the dual temptations of my overstuffed recliner and new TV subscription awaited. Better to spend another hour or so here going over the material. We had a podcast coming up next week, then the debate in a few weeks. I needed to be ready to talk about the issues.

The bell over the door rang, a reminder of the retail shop that once occupied this space. We really needed to lock the door and take that thing down, since we weren't open to the general public.

A voice filled the space. "Hello? Is anyone here? I heard this place is under new ownership."

My head shot up. I should hide. I would probably fit under my desk. Too bad the sound of my chair scraping back would probably give away my location. Maybe I should stay frozen in place, hoping the interloper would turn around and leave when no one answered his call.

Before I finished deciding how to react, a man stepped out of the shadows of the doorway, deeper into the room. The overhead lights illuminated his features, making it clear that I hadn't hallucinated that voice. He turned, eyes landing on me at my desk.

His eyes raked up and down my body in a way that gave me a different kind of shiver than it used to. "You look good, Mel."

"What are you doing here?"

My ex, Gary.

# Chapter Sixteen

**Seesaw:** Pole art imitates life. With this move, sometimes you're up and sometimes you're down....

*- Push and Pole Fitness Tutorials, Vol. 5*

My blood turned to ice water at the arrival of the man I'd last seen ripping the clothes off another woman. I'd tossed him out of my condo without a second thought (other than changing the locks) and hadn't heard from him in the weeks since. Typical that he would vanish without a trace and then show up at the worst possible time. It made no sense at all for him to be here.

His six-foot-frame filled the doorway. Since we'd broken up, he'd grown a full beard. Several inches of long, curly red hair, a riot that contrasted starkly with his buzz cut. His brown eyes carried the same trace of humor they always had, as if he couldn't be bothered to take anything seriously. When we were dating, Gary always seemed larger than life. Apparently the women he was seeing behind my back thought so, too.

Thoughts and emotions warred within me, all of them wrong. I didn't know what to say, how to act, what to think, where to be. Part of me wanted to stay seated at my desk, not moving or speaking, until Gary turned and walked away. Part of me wanted to yell at him for ruining my life. None of this would've happened if he hadn't burst in on me. I'd made plenty of videos for Dance 4 U, and the ones where I didn't land on my butt got about fifty views and maybe one or two new students for a few classes. Curtis and his mother never heard of me. Until this jerk made me go viral.

Part of me hoped this was a bad dream. Hopefully, I pinched the inside of my arm.

Ow. Nope.

At least everyone else was out. The only thing I needed less than my ex at campaign HQ was for the entire staff to meet him. I really didn't want to hear Erica's take on my poor decision-making.

"'What are you doing here?'" Gary repeated, in a bad imitation of me. "Is that any way to accept a compliment?"

I rolled my eyes. "Thank you for the compliment. What are you doing here?"

Grabbing him by the arm, I attempted to pull him out of the office, back onto the sidewalk. He dug his heels in. Using brute strength, I probably could have forced the issue, but I couldn't risk the possibility of any passerby seeing me bodily remove him from the premises.

Funny, sure. But not exactly the type of behavior one expects from a state senator. Erica would have a fit.

He planted his feet in place. "That's the greeting I get? No 'it's nice to see you?' What, am I not cool enough for your fancy new friends?"

"What are you talking about?" I hissed through clenched teeth.

"All the rich new politics people you're hanging out with," he said. "Yeah, I know whassup. You dumped me out of nowhere, and then you run for office. You think I wasn't good enough to be a state senator's man?"

This was unbelievable. How anyone could distort reality so much boggled my mind. "First of all, I didn't dump you 'out of nowhere.' We broke up for many reasons, including that you were cheating on me."

He shrugged. "Variety is the spice of life."

My hand itched to slap him. Only the knowledge that it would somehow get back to Erica—or worse, the press—stopped me. Closing my eyes, I forced myself to count to ten before I attempted to reboot this conversation. "How are you, Gary?"

"Great, Mel, thanks for asking. And you?"

"Oh, just dandy," I said through clenched teeth. "To what do I owe this unexpected pleasure?"

"I want to help with the campaign," he said. "They say it takes money to run for office, right?"

"You'd have to ask my manager," I said. "I'm not in charge of donations. Did you want to contribute to the campaign?"

"Yeah, I'll contribute. You help me out, and I won't tell everyone the things I know about you. Things that'll make you lose the election."

I rolled my eyes at him. "You don't know anything, Gary."

"I know that you dance around in your underwear in public."

"That's not news. Everyone knows that. Go away."

Footsteps alerted me to someone's approach, but I couldn't take my eyes off Gary. A moment later, Daniel appeared beside me.

"Hey," I said absently.

"Is everything okay?" Daniel asked.

"Aren't you going to introduce me?" Gary said loudly.

"No," I said. "You need to leave."

"I'm not going anywhere," he said. "You've got campaign funds, and I need money."

"I'm sorry," Daniel said. "Are you asking Melody to steal from her campaign and give it to you? In front of the person in charge of the campaign."

"Stay out of this, man. It's between me and my girl."

"Your girl. Right. What was your name again?" Daniel asked.

"Who wants to know?"

Ignoring him, I said, "His name is Gary Tribbiani."

"Like the guy on *Friends*?"

I shrugged.

"That makes it easy to remember," Daniel said. "Thanks."

"Hold up," Gary said. "Why do you need my name?"

"I'm happy to explain," Daniel said pleasantly. "You have fifteen seconds to get out of here or I'm going to call the police and report an attempted break-in at campaign headquarters. Then I'll ask them to come and cart you out of here."

The color drained from Gary's face. "You can't do that. Please, Mel, I'm desperate."

"Oh, I can," Daniel said. "I have a terrible memory, though, so if you leave now, chances are I'll forget your name around the time the door shuts behind you. Unless you bother Ms. Martin again."

They stared at each other for a long time. Gary was used to being the tallest guy in the room. Daniel had at least three inches on him, though, and he worked out. Finally, Gary shrugged. He stomped out. The door swung shut behind him with a joyful chime of the bell.

I didn't exhale until Gary moved beyond the enormous windows and out of sight. Then I went over and locked the door to ensure he couldn't come back. My legs shook. I was so grateful to Daniel for being there, for convincing my ex to leave that I could've kissed him.

He stood across the room, and suddenly that was much too far away. Closing the distance, I threw my arms around his neck and let out a whoop. "That was amazing!"

Daniel picked me up and spun me around. Our laughter filled the room. Then our eyes locked. He stopped moving. Slowly, he lowered me to the ground. He was everything. Daniel filled my eyes and ears and nose, and still I wanted more.

"Thank you so much," I said.

"You're welcome." The shakiness in his voice told me he was feeling the same desire that held me captive.

I leaned forward. The space between us evaporated. My lips touched his before either of us could stop to think. It was quick, so lightning fast I might have imagined it. But I didn't imagine the shell-shocked look on Daniel's face when he let go of me. I stepped back, dazed. Or the way I felt inside, all light and shimmery, like something magical was about to happen.

Except it wasn't. It couldn't.

"I'm sorry. I shouldn't…We shouldn't…" My face flamed. We'd talked about this. The two of us getting involved was a mistake. "I know, I know. Professional. I know."

"Melody—"

I wasn't even making any sense, but couldn't seem to stop talking. "No. I'm sorry."

"I've been wanting to kiss you since you pushed my car across that parking lot."

The flurry of words coming out of my mouth stopped instantly as I looked up at him. Suddenly, I couldn't breathe. "Oh. Me, too."

"But we can't," he said, taking a step backward. "Not while we're working together."

"I know we can't. And I can't even have this conversation right now," I said. "I'm sorry. Please talk about anything else."

Daniel looked like he wanted to argue, but instead he took a deep breath and did as I asked. "So that's your ex, huh? Charming guy."

I snorted. "Yeah. It's a shame things didn't work out between us."

"Are you okay?"

It wasn't until he asked that I realized my hands were shaking from the encounter. Gary had been kind of a weasel when we dated, but I'd never imagined that he would come to my work and try to extort money from me. "I will be."

"Come on. You should sit down. And we need to talk."

Daniel and I walked back into his office. I took my usual seat in front of his desk, but instead of moving around to his chair, he sat beside me. Our knees almost touched.

"When you first came in here, I asked if there was anything I needed to know about you," Daniel said. "Any dirty secrets?"

My head dropped into my hands. "Honestly, I thought Gary was long gone. I had no idea he would show up here. We broke up ages ago, long before that video."

"Were you dating long?"

"Off and on for about a year, maybe a year and a half. It was one of those things that didn't have a firm start or end date," I said. "A few months ago, I told him we were completely done when I caught him cheating on me."

"Ouch." Daniel winced. "I'm sorry. That always hurts."

"Thanks. I'm over it. But when that happened, I realized I'd been making the same bad choices over and over. It was time to take a break from serious dating, focus on myself. Then he busted in on me during that video, as the entire world saw. That pretty much confirmed every negative thought I ever had about him."

Daniel said, "So you don't still have feelings for him?"

"None. The more I think about it, the more I realize that our relationship was a mistake from the beginning. Dating Gary was easy. He didn't challenge me. I was lonely, and he knew how to make me feel special."

"That's good," he said. "I mean, not that you made a mistake. But that you're over him."

When our eyes met, my breath caught at the longing in his gaze. He had to be thinking about that brief, fleeting kiss. I certainly was. What it could've been if we'd let it continue. "Couldn't be more over him."

"Does getting involved with someone feel like a mistake now?"

This was such sweet torture. Never breaking eye contact, I shook my head. "Depends on the person. I know it's a bad idea, but getting involved with you feels like coming home."

"Every second I spend with you, all I want is to do this."

In an instant, he leaned forward. His lips captured mine, and I sighed with the sweetness and longing I tasted. His and mine, mingling. The kiss was hesitant, unsure. I returned it, knowing that we shouldn't but wanting to hold onto what I could. This wasn't like the brief kiss by the front door. That had been impulsive. This was deliberate, measured. This was the moment that we'd been building toward since I'd accidentally pushed his car into mine.

After a moment, he pulled back. My first instinct was to crack a joke. Deflect the tension. Excuse myself to go to the bathroom, get a glass of water. All the things I knew I should do. But I didn't want to. I looked up at him and almost gasped at the desire I saw in his eyes.

"You're not like anyone I've ever met," he said.

"Neither are you."

Daniel's hands cupped my face, and my hands buried themselves in his hair. A fire ignited inside me. I leaned out of my chair, trying to get as close to him as possible.

Somewhere outside, keys jingled. A moment later, the bell over the door rang yet again. Those sounds reminded me where we were. This wasn't the place for a stolen moment of passion. The two of us jumped, jerking apart as if someone fired a shot.

"Daniel? Are you still here? Why was the door locked?"

Oh, no. My heart plummeted at the familiar voice. Of all the people to catch us in the act.

Not wanting to believe, I turned and peeked through the cracked office door, toward the front of the building.

Erica was back.

# Chapter Seventeen

**Superman:** Make sure you have a spotter if trying this above the floor. The idea is to look like a superhero, with your thighs clamped around the pole and one arm stretched before you. The other holds you aloft…

*- Push and Pole Fitness Tutorials, Vol. 3*

Oh, man. Oh, no.

Erica couldn't catch us, not like this. Not after she and I spent half the day arguing about how I presented myself to the world. This was the worst possible moment for her to walk in.

"Shhh." Daniel smoothed back my hair. His lips hovered above my ear. "Slip into the bathroom. I'll head her off."

I nodded silently as he left his office and went to greet Erica. The bathroom was about four feet away, just to the left of Daniel's office. Barely breathing, I inched down the hall. A moment later, I eased the door into place behind me with a death grip on the knob to stop the metal from clicking. As soon as the latch silently fell into place, my breath returned. Almost home free.

The face in the mirror barely resembled me, all swollen lips and flushed skin. My hair was wild. Anyone who saw me couldn't doubt what I'd been up to, especially since Daniel's hair resembled mine before we'd gotten interrupted. He could claim he'd fallen asleep at his desk or something, but not when I looked as disheveled as he did.

I splashed water on my face, counting slowly until my heartbeat returned to its normal pace. Then I skinned my hair back into a ponytail to tame it, flushed the toilet to explain why I'd been standing in the bathroom for five minutes, and went out to give the best performance of my life.

"Hey, Erica. I thought you went home for the night."

"Too much to do," she said absently, scrolling through something on her phone. "You're still here?"

I cleared my throat, swallowing back a snarky response. "Yeah. Just thought I'd go for a run before heading home. Take advantage of the light while I can."

She nodded dismissively. "I'll see you tomorrow."

Just like that, I'd been spared. She hadn't even looked at me. Gary should be long gone, so I could take off through the neighborhood without fear of running into him. Things had been stressful, and truly, the physical release of getting some exercise would do me good.

Erica made it seem like the world would be watching me every time I stepped into public. While I didn't truly believe anyone cared about me that much, the very idea of constantly seeing members of the press everywhere I went made me not leave the house much other than for campaign business. Even at headquarters, Daniel had found enough staff to handle most of our daily needs. I largely went to lunches with donors, visited the local colleges, and tried to explain to people why they should vote for me.

Although I'd always been extroverted, the process of constantly begging other people for approval exhausted me. I missed my studio, my routine, my old life. The ability to invite men over if I wanted, without worrying about who might see them entering or leaving.

I missed being able to ask a man out on a date if I wanted. One man in particular. I missed being able to kiss someone new without worry about who was watching.

My feet pounded against the pavement. Running had never been my favorite activity, but being out like this felt amazing. I couldn't go to the studio. My local gym was half an hour from campaign headquarters, past my house. Most days, I didn't feel like driving out there. So, running. My frustrations melted a bit more each time my foot pounded my aggravations out against the pavement.

Erica. *Stomp.* Wearing my dress. *Stomp.* Ruining my hair. *Stomp.* Knowing that I couldn't be with Daniel. *Stomp.* The media, *stomp*, directing my life without even knowing they were doing it. *Stomp.*

I ran on and on, not paying attention to street signs, just wanting to keep moving until I felt like myself again. I turned right, then left, then right, knowing that my phone's GPS would lead me back to my car when the time came. Before I knew it, darkness fell, but I kept running in the glow of the street lamps.

Eventually, I drew to a halt. I didn't know the name of the street I'd turned onto, but it didn't extend very far. Ahead of me, the road dead-ended into a gate and a sign. That's not what caught my attention. Because standing in front of me, the streetlamp shining off of it like a beacon of hope, I spotted the most glorious thing I'd ever seen: a pole.

Not an actual fitness pole in the middle of the street; that would be ridiculous. At the end of the street lay a playground. A playground with swing sets and slides and platforms and a fireman's pole for children to play on. Children and fitness instructors, that is. My spirits lifted ten thousand percent. This was what I needed.

Barely able to contain my excitement, I hop-skipped across the distance until I was close enough to put my palms against the cool metal. I wanted to lean forward and kiss it, not even caring that it must be covered with germs from thousands of people.

After weeks away from the sport, I feared I wouldn't remember how to do anything. Just to see, I wiped my sweaty armpit on my shirt, clamped the pole between my right arm and my side, rested my right hip on the pole, and spread my legs into a perfect vee shape. My body fell into the teddy bear pose like I'd been born doing it.

With a tiny squeal of joy, I dropped to the ground and glanced around. No one else was in the park or the surrounding streets. Windows in the nearest houses were dark. This time of year, only masochists and hard-core fitness junkies wandered the streets after dark. No one would see me. I could manage a real workout, and Erica never needed to be any wiser.

The rest of the world dropped away. I swung, kicked, climbed, and inverted until I was dripping with sweat and panting. After several moves in a row left me breathing hard, I hooked my right leg and laid back to catch my breath, wiping strands of hair off my forehead. All the blood rushed to my head; it felt glorious.

When I hung from a pole, I was invincible.

I would win the election. The temporary injunction would expire, and Helen would be allowed to run her studio again. I'd be in a position to help other women whose businesses were threatened. Daniel and I would finally get a chance to have an honest talk about our feelings. Nothing could stop me now.

# Chapter Eighteen

**Basic Drop**: Do NOT attempt this move without a crash mat. Start from mid-pole until you've got the mechanics down, then move higher. To drop, do a basic climb, then move into a pole sit. Move your upper body around the pole like in a crucifix. With hands off the pole, open your legs.

*- Push and Pole Fitness Tutorials, Vol. 3*

Sirens blared, jolting me out of a sound sleep. Fire! I leaped to my feet, scrambling to find something to cover myself with. No time to get dressed. Any cover would do. I needed to get out.

Grabbing a pair of panties off the floor, I shoved one leg in. My foot slipped on the wooden floor, sending me back against the wall. With no time to waste, I hopped on one foot, trying to get my toes unstuck from the lace without face-planting.

The blaring stopped.

The sudden silence made me pause. Or at least, I tried. My momentum tipped me over. I crashed to the floor in a tangled heap.

Ten seconds later, my phone beeped. The voicemail notification. Hold on a sec.

Cautiously, I sniffed the air. Nothing but my vanilla bath bomb from the night before, still lingering. My phone started beeping on the nightstand. Oh, geez. Erica. I'd completely forgotten that, after our first meeting, I set her ring tone to the fire alarm so I knew not to answer. She usually texted instead of calling.

*Great move, Mel.*

My phone told me it was only six-thirty in the morning. My schedule for the day remained open until ten. Whatever Erica wanted, it could wait. Silencing my phone, I rolled back over. It started vibrating on the nightstand. What could she possibly want this early? Did she know what happened between me and Daniel? Well, if she did, she could yell at me later. It was way too early.

With a groan, I turned my phone off, dragged a pillow over my head, and rolled back over. In a few seconds, I was blissfully dreaming of life on the beach with a mai tai in one hand.

Sometime later, ringing woke me again. I grabbed my phone and chucked it at the wall, but the sound didn't stop. Probably because it was still off. In my sleepy haze, it took me a moment to recognize the doorbell. The clock on my nightstand showed that it was now six-fifty-three. Apparently, Erica didn't like being ignored.

Another groan escaped me. This had to be a bad dream.

*Please God, don't let Erica have tracked me down and come to ruin my morning.*

Things had been okay when we parted yesterday, and I

didn't think she figured out what Daniel and I were doing in his office when she showed up. If he'd told her after I took off, she would've called right away. Stewing in her anger for twelve hours didn't make any sense. Unless calling to wake me up was part of my punishment.

No. None of that made any sense. Daniel wouldn't tell her about our personal business, especially not before we got to talk about it ourselves. But I couldn't think of any other reason Erica would be standing on my doorstep, laying on the doorbell before the sun finished clearing the horizon. In February.

My brain urged me to leave her out there, let her freeze. Unfortunately, she wouldn't be here unless it was important. It would be easier to call her back, or text to see what she wanted, but at this point she'd just order me to come open the door.

Still grumbling to myself, I threw the covers back and got out of bed. I went to swipe a t-shirt off the floor to cover myself before remembering that I'd tossed everything in the dryer before going to bed the night before. Somehow, I doubted that Erica would feel like waiting patiently on the porch while I dug through my laundry for something to wear.

Grumbling at my bad luck, I yanked the bedspread around me as I stomped across the living room, wrapping it like a sari to cover my nudity. Meaning that when I opened the door to find Erica spitting rage from her eyeballs, the half dozen reporters camping out on the front walkway got quite an eyeful.

*Oh, balls.*

My entire body sagged against the frame as I processed the scene in front of me. So many people. Cameras. Flashes. And a cacophony of words coming at me. "What are you doing here?"

Behind her, a bald forty-something guy pushed his way to the front of the crowd and shouted at me. Jerry. I couldn't make any words out through my confusion. Not that I wanted to speak with him at the moment, standing shivering in my doorway wrapped only in a duvet.

"Don't just stand there." Erica hissed, shoving me out of the way. "Get inside! Close the door. And cover yourself. You're naked."

"I was sleeping." I moved aside enough for her to stride past me toward the kitchen, a briefcase swinging from one hand. After closing and locking the door while hopefully not letting the reporters take any more pictures, I followed her. "I sleep naked."

"What the hell were you thinking?"

"Good morning to you, too, Erica. Would you like some coffee? Is it okay if I get dressed before you start harassing me?"

"I'm not here to harass you, you idiot. Someone *saw* you!"

"That's what happens when you pull someone out of bed before seven a.m. banging on their front door," I said reasonably.

"Not the reporters waiting outside! Last night. In the park."

Realization slowly dawned. Someone spotted me poling. But who? And how did she know about it?

She slapped a newspaper down on the counter. There I was, plastered on the front. A gorgeous picture. Perfect form, legs split into a vee, with my toes pointed. Probably not the right focus. But it was on the tip of my tongue to ask if I could keep the image. It would make a great advertisement.

"Where did you get this?" I asked instead. The park had been deserted. Even if anyone saw a woman playing around, how would the media know it was me? Why would they care?

"Someone saw you. It's all over the news. You, doing exactly what I told you not to do. Hanging from a pole in a park at night. And not just any park," she continued, "but the only park in the area where drug dealers have reportedly been spotted."

"Oh, c'mon. There was no one in the park but me. Clearly, I wasn't dealing drugs. If you looked at the pictures, you know I was just having fun."

"But we talked about this! You can't have that kind of fun when you're running for public office. Especially not when it's only weeks until the election. Did you forget everything I ever said to you? Do you want to lose?"

That hurt. Usually, when Erica blustered, I ignored her, but the accusation that I would try to sabotage my own campaign stung. I flinched as if she'd slapped me. Then I turned and walked toward my bedroom.

"Where are you going?" she demanded.

"To shower," I said. "To put some clothes on. To give you a chance to calm down. Make some coffee. I'll be back in twenty minutes."

"Make it ten. We've got a lot of damage control to do."

I desperately wanted to talk to Daniel before Erica did, but calling him now wasn't going to resolve anything. In my tiny condo, she would easily overhear our conversation, and Erica did not need to know the details of my private life. Besides, he was probably as angry as she was. He might've even been the one to tell her about the papers. After all, Daniel was the one who wanted me to change my image in the first place.

What horrible luck. I couldn't believe my moment of weakness blew up in my face like this.

Part of me was tempted to linger, to make Erica wait, but she might call Daniel and tell him I wanted to get caught. Of course, I didn't. But a caged animal is going to escape when given the opportunity. They'd clipped my wings, but they couldn't take away my need to fly. That moment in the park was about me, not Erica or Curtis or my studio or the people of New York. Unfortunately, I couldn't afford to piss Erica off more by ignoring her ten-minute deadline. If she quit on me now, I'd lose the campaign.

We didn't have time to hire someone new, even if someone was available. I still needed her help. We needed to find common ground, figure out how to work together. And do to that, I did something I should've done about Erica earlier: I called my lawyer.

Lana answered her phone from a coffee shop where she'd already stopped to pick up breakfast. She promised to be on my doorstep, with chocolate croissants and lattes, in less than twenty minutes. I could manage Erica for a little while on my own, knowing backup was on the way. Especially after a long and fortifying shower.

When I returned to the kitchen full clothed with wet hair streaming down my back, newspapers lay spread across every surface. The original front page she'd shoved at me was there, along with several others, including a surprise spread from a New York City paper. Who knew they cared about our little election down there?

Erica sat on a stool at the island, sipping something steaming from a paper cup she must've brought with her. Good, because like an inconsiderate jerk, I didn't ask Lana to bring her anything. She spoke into her phone, back to me.

When I walked in, she said, "I'll call you back" and banged the phone onto the counter. To me, she said, "Daniel is very disappointed."

"You called my campaign manager?" *Please, please, please tell me he didn't mention the kiss.*

"Of course I did. He needs to know about the difficulties I'm having with this assignment. You should have spoken with him already."

"Yes, and maybe I would have if I'd been awake for more than thirty seconds before you barged in. Excuse me for thinking that maybe I should find out what the hell's going on before calling to report that there's a circus outside my front door."

"That circus isn't going to go away as long as you give them stories like this. Once you catch their eye as someone sensational or interesting, that's it. That's why I told you to be careful. But you didn't listen. And look at what happened." She gestured wildly at the pages all over my kitchen.

The first newspaper I picked up showed me hanging upside down, legs spread under a headline that read, STRIPPER RUNS FOR STATE SENATE by Jerry Turner. Hmmmph. He'd seemed so nice when he did my candidate profile after the fundraiser. I didn't even know what to say.

"But there was no one else around…" I said helplessly. It sounded weak, even to my own ears.

"The evidence establishes otherwise."

Behind me, the front door opened, then closed. A moment later, Lana appeared at my side. I gratefully accepted the hazelnut latte and chocolate croissant she offered, no longer feeling bad about not buying Erica anything. How dare she call Daniel without talking to me first? What did she say about me before I walked in? Was she trying to convince him to get me to drop out of the election? Or was he trying to stop her from walking away and leaving the campaign high and dry?

"Nice to see you again, Erica." Lana peeked around my arm at the pictures of me posing on the pole. "Wow. Great chopper!"

"Are you here to help?" Erica asked.

"To help you? No. I'm here to support Melody. Who is in kick-ass shape and likes to work out and isn't doing anything illegal or immoral."

"Well, there were signs saying the park closes at sundown," I admitted.

"Were you cited?"

"No."

"Then it doesn't matter."

"You're completely missing the issue at hand," Erica said. "My job is to make Melody likable so people will vote for her. Women running for office have an extraordinary challenge in this country. Look at Hillary Clinton. Look at Elizabeth Warren. It sucks, but we live in a world where a woman has to be twice as good as a man to get half as many votes. I've spent the last three weeks molding Melody into someone the people of Saratoga can respect enough to want her representing them." She jabbed her finger at the pictures. "How can people respect this?"

"You're not giving the voters enough credit," Lana said. "Maybe they'd respect Mel for being strong and passionate and believing in herself. Or for having the kind of dedication it takes to get to her level."

Erica snorted. My head swiveled back and forth between them. "You're hopelessly naive."

"You know what? You're fired." Lana said. "I can handle Melody's image from here."

My mouth dropped. Never in my wildest dreams had I expected this. But Daniel would object much less strenuously to my letting Erica go if I had someone else to step into her shoes. Lana was a lawyer; she had a background in politics. Maybe she didn't have Erica's specific experience, but she could handle the job.

"You can't fire me," Erica said. "I don't work for you."

"Maybe she can't, but I can," I said.

"No, you can't, either. I was hired by the party, paid by the campaign."

"Fine," I said. "I'll call Daniel and tell him to fire you. But for now, please leave."

Erica swept her briefcase off the counter and stormed out.

Newspapers fluttered around the room in her wake. As soon as the door slammed, I squealed and hugged Lana.

"Thank you so much!"

"You're welcome! I can't believe you put up with that bitch for so long," she said. "Now, first things first. Let's go to my place. I need a pole lesson."

# Chapter Nineteen

**Splash:** So named, presumably, because you look like you're about to fall face-first into a swimming pool. But gracefully. When I started pole, I learned so very many cool ways to fall…

*- Push and Pole Fitness Tutorials, Vol. 3*

By the time I finished my lesson with Lana, my spirits rose significantly. They plummeted again when I entered campaign headquarters that afternoon and found Erica and Daniel sitting in the back office, stone-faced. Apparently she was right, and I didn't have the authority to fire her. Darn it. I still hadn't gotten a chance to talk to Daniel about last night, and I'd stupidly hoped he would be alone when I got here.

He looked up when I entered, stone-faced. My heart plummeted. He definitely didn't look like he wanted to kiss me again. Whatever I'd hoped to say stuck in my throat. I looked around for anything to do other than going to join them. Our interns sat by the back wall in the main room, both speaking rapidly into the phone while other lines rang off the hook. Jade was speaking Spanish, while Seth spoke into the main office phone and texted on two cells simultaneously. Impressive.

Guessing why our phones suddenly became so busy, I didn't offer to help. Better to face the music and get it over with.

"What's going on?" I asked, the sinking feeling in the pit of my stomach already suggesting the answer.

"We've got some new data," Daniel said. "To be blunt, it's not good."

"Your little show in the park may have sunk this campaign," Erica said.

With a sigh, I sank into a chair at the end of the table. "What are you talking about?"

"We've been polling all morning," he said, "and your numbers are sinking like the Titanic. How could you do this?"

"I didn't do it to hurt the campaign," I snapped. "Finally, after weeks of acting like a dress-up doll, I took ten minutes to enjoy myself."

"I hope it was worth it," Erica said.

"It might have been, if you'd gone away like I told you."

"Sorry, Melody, but you can't fire Erica," Daniel said.

"I told her that." She glared daggers at me.

"Shut up," I said, crossing my arms over my chest.

"Ladies!" The sharpness in Daniel's voice hit me like ice water. Things were worse than I thought. "Erica, you're here to help Melody. If you're just going to antagonize her, go home. We can figure out how to fix things later. Melody, I know you didn't want to change your image, but Erica and I can help you win. Please, let us do our jobs."

The plaintive tone in his voice punched me in the gut. He was right. If I wasn't going to listen to my advisors, I was wasting my time. I might as well go home and start applying for new jobs because Curtis would walk away with the election without trying.

"I'm so sorry," I said. "It was mostly dark, there was no one around. I had no idea anyone could see me. I just needed to blow off some steam."

"People are always watching you," Erica said. "Curtis has been pissed since the moment you filed. He expected to walk into this position without breaking a sweat, and you took that away from him. Now he's looking for anything to make you look bad that won't be traced back to him. No one is just a random jogger. Assume everyone you meet may have been hired by the other side."

"Wow, that's paranoid."

"That's politics."

"How bleak."

"Hold on. We're getting ahead of ourselves," Daniel said. "Let's look at the numbers. Hard data, not accusations."

"I'm not making accusations, I'm providing information that Melody needs," Erica said. "She's clueless about all this."

"That's enough finger-pointing for now." He stepped between us, forcing us to take a step back. "It doesn't matter whose fault this is. We need to fix it."

"Thanks," I said.

"The good news is, you're up twenty-seven points with college-aged men and men over sixty-five." His lips twitched. "I mean, you do have some mad skills. Those pictures are—" He caught Erica's deathly stare and shook his head. "Never mind."

At least one of us found this amusing. It wasn't exactly breaking news that oversexed college boys and old men were turned on by a woman dancing on a pole. If anything, I'd have expected the numbers to be higher. I rolled my eyes, ignoring the flicker of hope that ignited at Daniel's comment. Now wasn't the time to discuss any skills I wanted to show him.

"What's the bad news?" I asked, hoping to get my mind back on track.

"The largest college in our district is a women's school. You polled fairly well with self-identified lesbians and bisexuals, but it's a small percentage of the total student body." I groaned, holding my head in my hands. "Still, thirty-seven percent of the women at Skidmore said they thought what you did looked 'cool', and they wish they had the upper body strength to try it.

"You've gone up eleven points with blue-collar men since the story went live. That helps with the northern part of the district. Unfortunately, you're down twelve points with women over twenty-three, and forty points with voters who identify as religious."

With each word, I wanted to cry more. "Is there any silver lining here?"

"Well, if you lose and open your own studio, you may get a lot of eighteen to twenty-three-year-old men traveling from Albany to take classes. The college students will be lined up around the block."

"That would be excellent news if losing the election didn't also mean Curtis would pass laws preventing me from working."

"Touché," Daniel said. "That's not the only problem. A lot of people who support you aren't planning to vote. It's tough to get college kids to the polls, especially for a non-Presidential election. We were always expecting low turnout, but Curtis gave a speech this morning on role models and 'appropriate conduct.' He was already slightly ahead as a known commodity, and now he's up close to nine points."

My heart sank. I needed to overcome a nine-point gap in just a few weeks. All because people didn't like something I did that had nothing to do with my politics. This world was bananas.

Erica said, "You'll have to issue a formal apology for trespassing and inappropriate public behavior."

My jaw clenched involuntarily. Inappropriate, my ass. "I'm willing to acknowledge that I shouldn't have been in the park after it closed."

Daniel leaned forward and placed one hand on my arm. I ignored the fireworks that shot down to the tips of my fingers. "Erica, issue an official statement from the campaign, apologizing for the incident and promising a donation to the City Parks Department."

She shot me a triumphant look that made me seethe even more. "Do you want to review the apology before I send it out?"

"I don't need to see it," Daniel said. "I trust you. You know what to do."

Unlike me. I didn't know what to do. All I did was ruin the campaign. They didn't trust me to help fix it. Daniel didn't believe in me. No one believed I could do this.

Blinking back frustrated tears, I rose to my feet. "Well, then, I guess you don't need me. I'm just the screw-up candidate."

As I stalked toward the door, Daniel called my name, but I ignored him. He didn't follow. Erica spoke in such a low voice I couldn't make out her words. It didn't matter.

I needed a way to fix things, to figure out how to fight back. If Curtis beat me, I would lose everything.

# Chapter Twenty

**Angel:** When you go into your climb, push off the ground with your foot to make the pole spin. Then, arc your left arm over your head, push your body through, right arm first, and spin.

*- Push and Pole Fitness Tutorials, Vol. 2*

After that, Daniel moved Erica from image consultant to Communications Director. That may or may not have meant they gave up on me as a lost cause. It probably included a raise. Her job didn't change much. She'd already been changing my look, handling press inquiries, and assisting with public appearances. Now she wrote speeches and stopped critiquing my outfits (most of which she'd picked out, anyway). As long as she left me alone, I didn't care if Daniel called her the Flying Spaghetti Monster.

After a couple of days, things largely died down, although

some reporter named Jerry kept posting old clips of the videos I'd done before that one went viral and changed everything. No idea how he found them, since they'd all been taken down after Curtis got the injunction. Guess it's true what they say: the internet is forever.

Daniel didn't mention our kiss, and neither did I. We seemed to have reached an unspoken agreement to forget it ever happened. Or at least to focus on the campaign for now. I called Lana, cried on her shoulder for about fifteen minutes, and then forced myself to let him go. With so many eyes on me right now, I just couldn't risk getting involved with my campaign manager. There was too much at stake. If it was meant to be, we'd figure something out when the time was right.

Every time another video appeared on the newspaper's website, I dropped another point and a half in the polls among those who planned to vote, rose three points among those who didn't. When each story broke, I half-heartedly suggested to Daniel we abandon all our plans and go beg the college kids to come out and vote since they liked me. But there weren't nearly enough of them. Most still used their parents' homes as their legal residences—and their registered voter addresses. The registration deadline was long gone. Only the commuter students would be part of the special election.

Late one afternoon, I was on the phone with a potential voter when the first wave of sneezes hit me. "Are you—achoo! —planning    to—achoo!—vote    in    the    special—achoo! —election?"

"Is everything okay? You know, you shouldn't be at work if you're sick. You could infect others."

Sniffling, I took a deep breath. "I'm so sorry about that. No, I'm not sick. There must be some dust in the air."

Weird that I would get a sudden attack, though. Usually I wasn't sensitive to dust or anything—achoo!

Appearing out of nowhere, Daniel handed me a tissue and took the phone out of my hand. "Thank you for your support, Mr. Upshaw. We'll have to call you back."

Another wave of sneezes hit me. When it subsided, my nose was streaming, and I could barely see. I grabbed for my water bottle to clear my throat, but it did nothing.

"Mel, if you're sick, go home," Daniel said. "There's a lot to do before the election, and not a lot of time."

"I know, and I'm so sorry." I sneezed again. "I don't know what's come over me. It's almost like—"

Erica stepped into view behind me, carrying a small white poodle under her arm.

"—someone brought a dog into the office."

"Oh, dear." Maybe the lack of oxygen reaching my brain made me overly sensitive, but it sounded an awful lot like Erica was feigning concern for my well-being. "Are you allergic to dogs?"

I nodded. When she didn't move, I tried to force words out between sneezes. "Can you—achoo!—take that—achoo! —outside?"

"Princess Sofia Sassypants is not a 'that,' she's a she," Erica said snidely.

"You named a dog?—achoo!" Never mind. This conversation could wait until I regained the ability to breathe.

Finally realizing that I wasn't putting on a show, Erica led the dog over to Jade while I stumbled into the bathroom to blow my nose about six hundred times and wash my face repeatedly. A few splashes of cold water helped me feel better until I looked up at the mirror. Even my mom wouldn't recognize me. My face was bright purple, eyes swollen nearly shut.

But at least I could breathe. Cracking the door open, I peeked out. Erica still stood by my desk, talking to Daniel, but the dog was nowhere to be seen. Jade must've taken her outside. I hoped she wanted to spend her afternoon with a puppy. Princess Sofia Sassypants couldn't stay in our office another minute.

"Sorry about that," I said when I returned. "I guess I should've mentioned at some point that I'm allergic to dogs."

"You're going to have to get shots," Erica said.

"What if you just don't bring your dog to work?" I shot back.

"Princess Sofia Sassypants isn't my dog, she's yours," Erica said.

"Excuse me?"

"I got you a dog," Erica repeated, as slowly as if speaking to a young child. "Poll results so far suggest that some people think you're a bit stiff, severe. People were having trouble relating to you."

Perhaps my ears were still clogged, but it sounded an awful lot like my Communications Director was telling me that I'd done too good a job of burying my real personality, on the advice of my image consultant—which was her—and that, as a result, people didn't want to vote for me. Because I was too good a robot.

Oh, the irony of it all.

"So you got me a dog? Without asking."

Daniel spoke up. "You know, I wouldn't have thought of it, but this is perfect. Did you know that almost every U.S. President in history has had a dog? People love dogs. When someone has a dog, it makes them seem relatable."

"That's beside the point. I'm allergic."

"Right. Not perfect. Sorry, I didn't know."

"No reason you should have," I assured him.

"We'll come up with something else," he said.

"No need." Erica didn't seem the least bit concerned that her plan was a bust. "As I said, they have shots. Princess Sofia Sassypants is perfect. Not only is she adorable, but she's sympathetic. When people see a woman who loves a three-legged dog, they instantly identify with her."

My heart skipped a beat. "Please tell me that you did not maim a dog to make people like me better. Please."

Daniel snorted, but he shifted his feet as if he wasn't sure he wanted to know the answer to my question.

"Don't be ridiculous! I've got a friend who works at an animal shelter, and I lucked out. Princess Sofia Sassypants is fully housebroken. You can take her to events with you. The purse was found with her, and they let me have it for a steal. After all, she fits perfectly."

Of course she did. Lana's voice rang in my ears. *Don't let them make the election about you. It needs to be about the issues.* Also, I didn't want a dog.

"Erica, if Melody is allergic, this isn't going to work. You should have asked her before getting her a dog."

"It's too late now. Princess Sofia Sassypants needs a home."

"She can't come with me," I said. "Even if I weren't allergic, my condo doesn't allow them."

Erica waved one hand. "That's not a problem. Emotional support animals are exempt from no pets' restrictions under the Fair Housing Act."

This was beyond ridiculous. I put my hands on my hips and glared at her. "You want me to tell people that I need an emotional support animal to help them relate to me better? You're standing here telling me to commit a fraud on the people who I want to represent as an elected official?"

"Of course not," she snapped. "Obviously, having a dog would benefit you emotionally. Studies find that pets are extremely beneficial to a person's mental health."

"Except for the tiny issue where I can't breathe when I'm within ten feet of one."

"Okay, fine, we'll do something else. Maybe you could donate her."

Daniel and I exchanged a glance. Maybe Erica had been working too hard. "What kind of place takes animal donations?"

She threw up her arms. "I don't know, the SPCA? Do I have to think of everything?"

"No," I said quickly. I couldn't have a dog, but sending her back to the shelter didn't seem like the answer. "No, you definitely don't need to handle this more. Thanks for the dog, Erica. I'll work something out."

"You know what? I'll take her for now," Daniel said. "I love dogs, and I have a big fenced-in yard where she can run around. We'll find a permanent solution later."

Instantly, I relaxed. It felt good to remember that he was on my side. "Thank you so much. I really wish I could, but there's no way."

"It's no problem."

Daniel went outside to relieve Jade from doggie duty. Through the window, I watched him crouch down as Princess Sofia Sassypants sniffed his face. She licked his mouth, and he laughed. The princess jumped onto her back legs, hopping up and down. She really was an adorable little thing, with her curly white fur and pointy little ears. Too bad I could barely see her with my eyes still swollen to slits.

I couldn't believe this was my life now. All because my stupid ex burst into my condo at the worst moment. If I hadn't fallen, about eleven people would have watched that promo video. I wished I'd never met Gary.

Unfortunately, wishing wasn't going to help me breathe. Antihistamines would. After a quick trip down the street to buy some allergy medication, I felt largely human again. By the end of the day, my sinuses had almost returned to normal, and Daniel had made a new best friend.

Things at campaign headquarters became more strained.

Erica did her job, but her growing disdain made me wonder just how much she made that she was willing to stick around. She'd clearly be happier working anywhere else.

# Chapter Twenty-One

**Flatline**: To start, do a basic climb. Sit with the pole clamped between your thighs and your legs extended in front of you. Lean backwards, pushing outward against the pole below your body. Remove your top arm from the pole, extending it over your head.

*- Push and Pole Fitness Tutorials, Vol. 2*

Days turned to weeks until finally, we made it to the Thursday before the election. Daniel and I hadn't kissed again. The playground incident cooled things between us. Yes, I'd given in to temptation. But it had been a rough and stressful few weeks; I deserved a chance to blow off some steam. Hopefully we could have a long talk once this was all over. Maybe go out for coffee.

We'd reached the home stretch. The final leg of the campaign—which meant, the time had come to face off against Curtis in a debate. This event could change everything.

If Curtis attacked me personally, attacked my morals, it would be hard to keep my cool. I'd been practicing, but it wasn't easy.

Lana's voice rang in my head: *Don't let them change the conversation. Keep it about the issues, not you.*

I didn't just get dressed, I armed for battle.

Even without my seven-inch platforms, I'd tower over my nemesis. My perfectly-applied, extremely natural-looking make-up gave me the strength of armor. Thank you, YouTube. I wore the most expensive suit Erica picked out for me with a red silk top just peeking out through the buttons. Robyn returned to the scene of the crime to fix my hair. Since she'd given me extensions, I didn't have to worry about more helmet head. Instead, she gave me a severe up-do that rivaled Erica's. A few well-placed tendrils softened the look, made it more me. Precisely what I asked for.

Before all this started, there had rarely been a need to dress professionally, but now I'd become a pro. Curtis wouldn't find any fault with my appearance tonight. No cleavage, no short skirts, no heels. Just me, pants with leg creases sharp enough to cut glass, and a blessed lack of shoulder pads.

When Daniel knocked on my door at exactly six-thirty, I was pacing inside the door. A glance at the time made me feel a little better. Punctuality was such a turn-on for my inner military brat. No matter what happened, at least we'd be on time.

The door swung open to reveal Daniel dressed in a gorgeously-tailored dark gray suit with a green shirt that brought out flecks I'd never noticed in his hazel eyes. For a heartbeat, I let myself imagine he was picking me up for a date and not to work on debate prep in the car.

"Hey," I said with a big smile.

"Hey. You look gorgeous." He stepped forward and kissed my cheek, which sent a jolt through me. "If this were a beauty contest, you'd win for sure."

"I don't know about that. I bet Curtis looks pretty good in a swimsuit." I gave him a teasing smile.

"True, but you'd knock 'em dead at the talent portion."

"Damn right."

We both laughed, and instantly I felt calmer. Daniel opened the car door for me, a chivalrous gesture that some people found outdated but that secretly thrilled me.

After settling into the driver's seat, he leaned over and squeezed my hand. "Ready?"

"As I'll ever be," I said. "Thank you so much for doing this."

"You'll be great. If all else fails, when Curtis gives an answer, respond with 'Everything that guy just said is bullshit.'"

I laughed, recognizing the line from one of my favorite old movies. "I'll keep that in mind."

"And don't worry about slut-shaming. I may have hinted that if Curtis drags your reputation through the mud again, I'll out him to the press."

I gasped. No way. "You wouldn't."

"Of course not. But Curtis doesn't know that. He's so wrapped up in the idea of making his mother proud—and restoring the family's image—he's lost sight of who he is. And we need this debate to be about the issues affecting the people of New York, not his mommy issues."

When we arrived at the high school gymnasium where the debate was being held, Erica waited behind the wings. She looked perfect as ever, in a navy blue suit cut similar to mine and two-inch kitten heels.

Her beady eyes swept me up and down before she said a word. "I guess that'll do."

"Aw, jeez, Erica, talk like that's going to make me blush."

"Sarcasm does not befit a senator."

Since she wouldn't approve of any of the responses I had to that statement, I turned to examine the auditorium. It looked quite a bit like the debate stages I'd seen on TV, except there were basketball hoops on either end of the room and bleachers instead of chairs for the audience. Two reporters set up video cameras around the stage, both from local stations. I didn't recognize either of them. Curtis and I weren't exactly MSNBC material, and that was okay with me.

"Remember to stick to the issues," Erica said. "No personal attacks on Curtis. Try not to mention his family unless he does. If so, stick to the facts. Former Senator Baker resigned his post in the middle of the term, abandoning the people, to pursue personal gain. You would never do that."

"But really, it's better to avoid your personal lives completely," Daniel added. "After all, Curtis started this whole thing by getting personal. You don't want to stoop to his level. If it comes up, change the subject."

"Got it." I took a deep breath. "Does anyone have a paper bag? I'm going to throw up."

"I thought you were used to performing in front of an audience," Erica said. Her tone revealed nothing, so I decided to do us both a favor and read it as supportive.

"Sure, but none of those big crowds ever cared what I had to say. Those were exhibitions or competitions."

"So is this," Daniel said. "Remember that."

His words gave me strength. My spine straightened, my head went up, and my shoulders dropped. Just another competition. I loved competing, and more than that, I loved to win. I would beat Curtis, just like I beat Shyla Turner, three-time New York state pole champion.

Across the room, the back doors opened, and Curtis entered with his mother and an older man I assumed to be his campaign manager. I nodded at them. "Does he bring his mom to all these events?"

"Well, it is her agenda he's pushing," Daniel said. "The Curtis I used to know wasn't nearly this conservative."

That certainly fit with the woman I'd met at the governor's

benefit. So annoying that the man who'd ruined my life wasn't even doing it on his own behalf, but to please his mother. I turned to ask Erica what she knew about the Baker family, but she'd melted away, vanishing into the crowd.

"Are you okay for a minute?" Daniel asked. "I need to check on something."

I nodded. Having him around brought me strength, but my campaign manager had a lot of things in his job description other than keeping me calm.

People filled the high school gymnasium, trickling in slowly as the clock ticked ever closer to the starting time. When the little hand finally neared the twelve, Daniel returned and handed me a small bottle of water. The thoughtfulness touched me.

The moderator, Karen, sat down and explained the rules. She looked like a soccer mom, which made sense because Erica had told me she was the president of the local school board. She had that special haircut identifying her as the type of mom who never hesitated before asking to talk to a manager.

Curtis had won the coin toss earlier, so he took the stage first, introducing himself in a few words. At this point, his voice set my teeth on edge, so I kept my face neutral and tried to block him out, clapping politely when he stopped.

When I spoke, my voice was clear and strong. Erica's prepared words sat on notecards lying on the podium in front of me. "Good evening, everyone. Thank you for coming out tonight to talk to us. My name is Melody Martin, and as you know, I'm running for state senate. I believe in freedom of expression, personal liberties, and supporting each other."

The audience clapped politely, which was about as much as I could expect. If they clapped more or less for Curtis, I couldn't tell. They'd cheered Karen warmly when she entered, but she'd apparently had kids in this school for the past seventeen years and knew every parent in town.

She asked Curtis the first question, a relative softball about whether he planned to raise property taxes. (Spoiler alert: of course not!) He cleared his throat, and we were off to the races. Unfortunately, not literally. In a footrace, I could absolutely beat Curtis. Even if I'd been allowed to wear my heels.

About half an hour into the debate, I felt like I was holding my own. A lot of the questions were exactly what Erica had prepared me to expect: how did I feel about raising the minimum wage, about paid sick leave, about mandatory health care. Having lived in multiple foreign countries with my parents growing up, even though we'd been on military bases, I saw the benefit of all of those things. It was easy to talk about my life experiences, and the more I did, the more heads bobbed in the audience. People were relating to me. Even Erica wore a small smile, which for her was like if anyone else started doing jumping jacks in the aisle. Dare I say she might be proud of my performance?

Then Karen turned to me. "Ms. Martin, your opponent has mentioned his military service several times so far this evening. As you know, since the time of the American Revolution, this area has prided itself on being patriotic."

I knew no such thing. Could a Senate district be patriotic? No idea, but parts of *Hamilton* took place here, so maybe that was close enough. My head tilted as I waited for her to get to the point.

"What would you say to those voters who question your lack of military experience?"

Clearing my throat, I said, "I'm a military brat, Karen. I grew up on bases, traveled the world with my parents. My father is preparing to retire soon. My mother has a few years left. They have more than fifty years of combined service. No one supports the military more staunchly than I, and no one could more passionately argue the benefits of service."

From the look on Curtis's face, this part of my life story was news to him. He needed better researchers; it wasn't exactly a secret. I wondered how he'd planned to come after me on this issue. Score one for Team Mel.

I continued, "By the time I became old enough to enlist, I'd realized that my contributions to society would be more valuable in other areas. I craved the type of roots I couldn't get when being reassigned every couple of years, so I went to college, settled in the Capital District, and bought a home. I hope to one day start a family here."

The audience members clapped. Several heads nodded. They liked me!

Beside me, Curtis snorted. "When you talk about 'contributions to society,' does that refer to the time spent dancing naked in front of strangers?"

Oh, no he didn't. This debate wasn't supposed to get personal. Daniel promised. My face flamed. In the crowd, someone gasped. Karen coughed, and it looked as if she may want to hide a smirk behind her hands.

*I'd like to speak to your supervisor, Karen. You're supposed to be impartial.*

Determined not to let him get to me, I forced myself to count slowly to five. My eyes scanned the audience. Curtis would not feel the full force of my exasperation, and neither would our moderator. Attacking either of them would only make me look bad. No one would care that he'd started it.

My gaze fell on Daniel, sitting in the front row, beaming at me with pride. He didn't look shocked or disappointed in me at all. He flashed me an encouraging smile. Behind him sat a row of young women, probably students at the high school.

I didn't know what they were doing here, but they looked enthralled. One of them gazed up at me like I was the most important person in the world. She made me feel like a superhero. I smiled at her, and she waved.

"Ms. Martin?" The moderator asked, drawing me back to the moment. "Did you have a response?"

To my surprise, I found I did have something to say, other than, "Curtis is an ass." Which I did want to say, very badly, but I refrained.

No matter how frustrated I felt, this election wasn't about me. I had decided to run so other people could freely express themselves, run their businesses without the government turning into the morality police shutting them down. So young women like those in the audience could grow up, find their confidence, and be whoever they wanted to be. Votes mattered. Elected representatives mattered. Young people needed to see that men couldn't force women to live by their values anymore. Those days were gone.

My spine straightened. I said, "We all have our own gifts. We all contribute in different ways. Some people create art with their hands, sculpting or painting or writing books. Some people create art with their voices, singing or chanting. Dancing is just another form of art. It's beautiful. The fact that you personally aren't capable of opening your mind enough to enjoy something doesn't make it worthless.

"I'm proud of what I do. I'm proud of the joy I bring others. No one should be shamed into feeling that they need to hide their gifts, or who they are. A vote for me is a vote for individuality, for feminism, for being true to yourself."

The audience clapped. A couple of people whistled, although one of them might have been Lana, sitting near the back. I suppressed a smile, wondering what Erica thought of that.

Beside me, Curtis sniffed. "Yeah, I suppose you're an excellent role model for young girls everywhere. Dancing naked, sleeping your way to the top…Have I forgotten anything?"

The comment took me by surprise. Sleeping my way to the top? I couldn't remember the last timeS I'd even been on a date, much less more. "I have no idea what you're talking about, Curtis. My dance ensembles cover more than most two-piece swimsuits."

"So you're not sneaking around with your campaign manager?" He reached inside the podium and pulled out two pieces of paper. One in each hand, he held them up to the crowd.

Not documents, photographs. My gut clenched at the realization.

In the first, Daniel and I stood in a parking lot. My terrible hairdo identified it as the night of the first fundraiser. He whispered in my ear, one hand on my elbow. Thinking about that touch, I shivered. We did look intimate. I wanted to say that nothing happened, that the picture was a lie, but upon seeing the other, I knew there was no point. I had no idea why anyone had been following me, or what was happening, but—there it was. In full living color. Indisputable.

The second picture was shot through the front windows at headquarters, right after Gary left. I didn't know how anyone got close enough to get a good shot without us noticing them, but we'd been preoccupied. The how didn't matter: There we were. Me and Daniel, in that impulsive, stupid kiss. The one that led to our amazing, heart-stopping moment in his office.

A mistake. Which we'd both agreed not to tell anyone about or to repeat.

Fat lot of good that did me.

How...? Gary. It had to be Gary. The kiss happened right after we threw him out of the office. He must've come back. I didn't know why he would do that, but it didn't matter. Once again, my ex had found a way to ruin everything.

With no idea what to say, I turned to look for Erica. She must be so disappointed with me. She no longer stood at the edge of the stage where I'd last seen her, and for a moment, I feared that she was so upset, she'd finally abandoned me. Sure,

I didn't like her, but for all our differences, Erica was good at her job. Suddenly I wished I'd spent more time listening to her and less time resenting her. Maybe then this wouldn't be happening.

After a moment, my gaze landed on Daniel. His face was white. When he saw me looking at him, he shook his head slightly as if to say, "Don't engage." That's what Lana had been saying all along. Don't let them make the campaign about me. Force them to make it about the issues.

When I didn't respond, Curtis said, "Want to tell me more about your impeccable morals, Ms. Martin?"

My hands tightened around the edges of the podium, turning the knuckles white. I couldn't believe it. Everything I worked for meant nothing. Talking about the issues was a waste of breath. Not when all anyone wanted to do was slut-shame me.

Then I realized: slut-shaming *was* the issue. It was high time I addressed it head-on.

"Morals aren't about what you do for a living. It's not about what you wear. It's about how you live your life and how you treat people." I pointed at him. "And if we're judging people by how they treat others, I am not the one who should be ashamed of their behavior here."

A strangled sound escaped Curtis. I found Daniel again, worried that he'd be mad at me for not changing the subject like he'd suggested. Instead, he was laughing. Then he gave me two thumbs up, giving me the courage to square my shoulders and continue with what needed to be said.

"I'd have thought the lesson is to not use your office as a hotel room," Curtis said. "At least not without covering the windows first."

"You are so one-note. You know what? If the only thing you have to offer the people of Saratoga is that you don't like a woman who is confident in her sexuality, it's a waste of my time to stand here and act as your punching bag." I took a deep breath. "Thank you, Karen, for moderating. I think we've all seen enough."

Ripping off my microphone, I turned and strode out of the room. Erica looked as if I'd slapped her when I stormed past, but she didn't move to stop me. Good thing, because I would've mowed her over.

I made it halfway to the parking lot before realizing that Daniel drove me here, leaving me with nowhere to go. My feet skidded to a halt on the pavement. Lana was around somewhere. She would take me home. I couldn't face anyone. And I couldn't stand here until one of the reporters covering the debate came out with questions. I'd said enough inside.

Spinning around, I headed for Lana's car. Whether she expected to find me there or not, she'd certainly give me a ride.

The gym doors clanged open behind me. Holding my head high, I walked faster.

"Melody, stop!"

I should've known he'd come after me. With a heavy sigh, I turned to face him.

There was only one thing to say. "How?"

"I don't know," Daniel said.

A hollow laugh escaped me. "All that time I spent fighting the attraction between us. Guess I shouldn't have bothered. Turns out, there was no need for an image consultant, either. I let myself feel something for five seconds, and it's all over."

"This is fixable. But you've got to go back in there and finish the debate."

"No way." I shook my head. "Not happening."

"You can't leave."

"What does it matter? I'm losing. People hate me, remember? They hate me so much, Erica tried to give me a three-legged dog."

"I strongly suspect you made more than a few new fans

tonight. If you walk away now, Curtis wins."

"Then I guess Curtis wins. I was never the 'right' candidate, anyway, and we both know it."

Behind him, the doors to the auditorium opened again, and people trickled out. People who carried cell phones that made recordings that sometimes got posted on the internet and went viral. I couldn't have that happen. Not again.

"Can we please talk about this somewhere else?" he asked. "Or at least lower your voice. I don't want anyone to hear us."

"Of course no one should overhear us." My voice grew louder, nearly hysterical. "You wouldn't want to spoil the perfect image you created! Perfect Melody, the perfect candidate for state legislature. An empty vessel, with no thoughts or feelings of her own."

He stepped closer, reaching for me as if to calm me with his touch. "You know it's not like that. I was doing my job. Trying to get you elected."

As much as I appreciated the effect he'd always had on me, right now, I didn't want to be calm. I stepped backward. "By turning me into someone no one recognized?"

"By turning you into a winner. You're a fighter. I didn't create that; I didn't change it. You've got fire. It's what drew me to you in the first place."

My voice cracked. "Ironic, isn't it? Because you being drawn to me is what's going to make us lose."

"I don't care about winning anymore," he said. "Mel, please. I don't want you to give up because of one jerk."

"Yeah, well I care. Remember? If Curtis wins, Dance 4 U can never reopen. I won't be allowed to open my own studio unless I move. This is the only job I have, the only thing I know. And it's gone."

"I forgot. I got so caught up in winning, taking back the majority in the senate after so long…I'm sorry." His voice shaking, he said, "I love you."

I shook my head sadly. "Which me do you love? Mel the Pole Dancer? Or Melody the Politician?"

"What are you talking about?" He raked his fingers through his hair. "They're both you."

"I'm not sure that they are," I said. "I told you upfront that I didn't want to change who I am, and you insisted you didn't want that, either. But I can't help wondering. Would anything ever have happened between us if I'd declined Erica's assistance and walked away from this whole thing?"

"Maybe?" he said. "I liked you. When you walked into my office that morning, my whole day brightened. Maybe once I knew who you were, I would've asked you out. But we'll never know, because that's not what happened."

Great. We'd never knowf because I'd let myself think any of this was a good idea. I should have insisted on being myself from the start, to win or lose with my head held high. I hated that I let everyone shame me. I ripped my jacket off, opened the top buttons of my blouse.

"What are you doing?"

"Trying to find myself. See who is left underneath these stupid stiff clothes and layers of makeup."

"Stop. You're making a scene."

I threw my hands up in frustration. "And that's all you care about, right? Staying under the radar, not making waves? Every time my true self shone through, even a little, you'd back away. This was never about me. It was about creating the perfect Stepford candidate."

"If that's what you think of me, then it's probably good that we can't be together." He turned and walked away, shattering my heart.

All the words left me. I watched him go, mouth moving, with no sound. When he moved out of sight, my face crumpled. No longer caring if anyone saw, I sank to my knees on the pavement and let the tears flow.

# Chapter Twenty-Two

**Phoenix:** Before you attempt this move, make sure you can do a Chopper and Twisted Grip. As the name suggests, your body's going to be rising like a Phoenix from the ashes. Take it slow at first to avoid injury.

*- Push and Pole Fitness Tutorials, Vol. 4*

The conservative news outlets declared Curtis the winner of the debate, probably because I left. The liberal media swore it was me for refusing to deal with his abuse and walking out. Reading the evaluations and the comments online made my head hurt. None of it gave me any real insight into how I was doing.

Over the weekend, I turned into a bundle of nervous energy. A cranky bundle of nervous energy. The day after the debate, I avoided Daniel by texting that I wasn't feeling well and staying home. He and Erica had the campaign running just fine without me, and there wasn't much I could do in the way of damage control. He didn't call or text me back, and I left him alone. The election was in a few days, and at this point, we didn't have much left to say to each other.

I needed to slowly accept the possibility that our relationship had been doomed from the beginning. We were too different, and our budding attraction couldn't survive the stress of a campaign, especially not one that required me to do a total *My Fair Lady*. Turned out, the poised, polished Eliza Doolittle couldn't completely shed her inner flower girl. Not in the internet age.

I never should've let Curtis get under my skin in the first place. Sure, someone with his narrow views shouldn't be in politics making laws to oppress women. But somewhere along the line, I lost myself. I didn't need Erica. If people would support a candidate for president with a wife who used to model naked, why couldn't they support a pole fitness instructor for state senate. We were strong women, confident in our sexuality, and that shouldn't be a weapon against either of us. Men who ran for election weren't judged on "likability" or what they did in their free time; women shouldn't be either.

Between Curtis's attacks and Erica's impossible expectations, I'd lost myself. My job didn't define me. Whether I taught pole at the local dance studio or sat as the newest member of the New York State Senate, I was the same Mel Martin on the inside. That's what I'd forgotten.

Unfortunately, a return to the old Mel wouldn't solve any of my problems: Curtis would win the election, he'd convince the legislature to ban pole fitness, and if I wanted to teach, I'd be forced to give up the first place I'd ever called home for longer than a couple of years.

Sure, my family had lived in lots of interesting places. I'd seen and experienced more cultures in my teenage years than a lot of people did in their entire lives. I'd learned to cook a dozen cuisines from all over the world. I'd loved all of it, but at the same time, I longed for a place to call my own. Put down roots. That's what I thought I'd done here, but if I couldn't teach here, I'd have to move on. Again.

At least if I moved, knowing Daniel and I couldn't be together would hurt less. I couldn't believe I let myself fall for someone who only liked the person he changed me into. Our chemistry was undeniable, but once you took away the physical attraction, I needed someone who liked me for me. Even if he apologized, how could I know he wouldn't do it again?

Lana had to work over the weekend, so I borrowed her keys and spent several hours using her home studio, behind closed blinds, trying to work through my sorrow and frustration. I wound up sore and tired, but no closer to finding a solution.

Monday morning, Daniel asked me to meet him at HQ early, before everyone else showed up. Weird, but not entirely unexpected. Curious whether he intended to quit on me at the last minute, I thought about refusing. "What's the point? Haven't we already lost?"

"Please, Melody? I'd really like to talk to you."

The plea in his voice tugged at my heartstrings. As tempting as it would be to spend the day in hiding, licking my wounds, I couldn't let our argument after the debate be the last time I ever saw him without the entire staff around.

"Okay. I'll be in soon."

He waited for me in his office, in the back room that once belonged to the store manager. Ammunition catalogs remained stacked in the corner, making me wonder once again what happened to the people who used to rent this place. They seemed to have left a lot of random stuff behind. Like the giant deer head on the wall. Daniel refused to take it down, which represented the reason I rarely came into his office unless I had to.

He motioned to the empty chair across from his desk. "Good morning. Have a seat."

"Do I have to? That thing is looking at me."

"You mean Curtis?"

I looked around the empty office before drawing the obvious conclusion. "You named a stuffed deer's head after my opponent?"

He shrugged. "I had to call it something."

"What's going on, Daniel?" I asked when it appeared he wasn't in a hurry to enlighten me. Surely he didn't invite me here to talk about the latest in taxidermy developments.

"We've been doing some research, and I wanted to share the results with you."

"Sure. No problem."

Research results seemed like the type of information that could've been conveyed by email, but maybe it was so top-secret, he didn't want it in writing. Politicians could be weird like that.

"As you know, we do a lot of polling," Daniel said. "We call registered voters, ask what makes them vote for someone, what makes them *not* vote for someone. Early results showed that people thought you were charismatic and seemed trustworthy. Older voters were unsure about voting for Curtis after what happened with his father."

"You know, as much as I want him to lose, that doesn't seem fair."

"Fair or not, that's what the voters said. You were holding your own."

"And then after those pictures were viral, we lost points, right?"

"Right. I've spent a lot of time trying to figure out how to regain that ground," Daniel said. "I asked Erica to work with you because I knew the public's perception of women in your line of work—not to mention, of female candidates in general.

After the first couple of public appearances, you polled well. People thought you seemed genuine, down-to-earth, someone they could relate to."

"If only the election had been held on Valentine's Day," I muttered. Or if only I'd never gotten this hare-brained idea in the first place. There must be better ways to stand up for free expression and women's liberation.

He snorted. "I wish. Your numbers have been going straight downhill ever since the park incident."

I sighed. "I apologized for that a hundred times."

"To me, sure. Never to Erica. The campaign issued a public apology, but it didn't come out of your mouth. Some voters are upset that you never went on the record acknowledging your mistake."

"I didn–"

"Well, technically, you were trespassing," Daniel said.

Unfortunately, he had a point there. Arguing for the sake of arguing did nothing for me, so I conceded. "Fine. I'll apologize for that. Set it up."

"It's too late," he said. "Curtis has someone dogging you, posting your every misstep. Reposting the original viral video that caught his attention."

That stupid video again. I resisted the urge to smack myself in the forehead. "So what you're saying is, this is all my ex-boyfriend's fault?"

"Maybe. If not you, Curtis would have found someone else to go after. Personally, I'm glad you made him sweat a little. But that's beside the point. You came onto his radar, and now Curtis is taking every opportunity to reinforce his narrative."

"That's ridiculous!"

"I know that and you know that," Daniel said. "None of this is your fault, but we're talking about public perception. People care more these days about jumping to conclusions and waving pitchforks than facts. Fake news equals click rates equals ad revenues. It's all about sensationalism. When something big happens, it's essential to draw first blood, to get your spin out there first. We missed our chance to do that."

"So what do we do now?"

"Erica's been out there, working to put the record straight," Daniel said. "But the problem is these numbers from the weekend. The public doesn't think apologizing would help. The press has done a real number on you, and a lot of our core group of voters say they won't support you. They'd rather stay home tomorrow."

My head dropped to the desk. "So that's it? The election is over? I'm going to lose and Curtis is going to get my business shut down, and I'm left with nothing?"

In the beginning, the one high point in all of this had been the time spent with Daniel. Schmoozing and getting to know him while traveling in circles that he could show me how to navigate. The two of us growing closer as I tried to charm the people of my district. But even that silver lining turned out to be fleeting.

My heart ached.

This had all been for nothing. All the fights and the aggravation and the time I could've spent looking for my own studio space or advertising lost on creating the perfect, now useless, politician's wardrobe. Expensive clothes I probably couldn't return—especially not the ones I'd spilled food on. All the missed workouts and the classes. Time wasted plotting and campaigning that would've been better used doing anything else.

"Don't give up just yet," Daniel said. "We've got all day to think of something."

"Something other than reminding everyone that they voted for Mr. Baker and he ditched them to join a pyramid scheme after leaving his wife of forty years?"

"Well, yes, preferably. This election isn't about Mr. Baker.

And it shouldn't be about his personal life or yours." He pushed away from the desk, pacing under that stupid deer. "There's nothing wrong with being a fitness instructor. Americans love the gym, they love taking fitness classes, they love buying three-thousand-dollar exercise bikes. They also love instructors.

"The problem is, elections and media aren't about truth anymore. They're all about entertainment. And, unfortunately, what the media finds entertaining is dragging you through the mud, repeatedly."

Ugh. I took a big gulp from my coffee. "Our society sucks."

"Agreed." He continued pacing.

"Can we sue Curtis? What he's doing isn't right."

"It's not right, but it's unfortunately also not illegal. You're a public figure now, and that gives him a little more latitude."

"Why doesn't the press follow Curtis around?" I grumbled. "He can't be totally squeaky clean."

Daniel's lips twitched upward into a smile. "Because you're much more interesting than he is. For one thing, you're new. New is always more exciting. Everyone knows Curtis. But also, you're not afraid to be yourself, even with experts helping you tone down. You don't apologize. Curtis is a boring, cookie-cutter charming politician. He's a used-car salesman with a trust fund."

"A used car salesman with a trust fund...who secretly commits financial crimes? Maybe a bit of insider trading? I hear that's a big thing with politicians now. Come on, he's got to have a deep, dark secret somewhere."

Daniel shook his head. "The guy's a Boy Scout. Literally. He made Eagle Scout. Besides, I've run a clean campaign. Most of the things hurting us aren't his fault."

Part of me suspected that wasn't entirely true. Curtis easily could have asked the media to follow me or tipped them off as to what I did for a living. After all, it was his objection to my occupation that got us into this mess in the first place. If he'd simply stumbled across the video of me falling on my butt, laughed, and moved on like the rest of the world, I'd be at home right now working on new combinations for my advanced classes.

The tiny bubble of hope I'd started to nourish burst. "Is there anything I can do?"

Daniel shook his head. "At the moment, I don't know. I just wanted some time…it was selfish of me, but I wanted to see you, alone, before everyone else got here. You might as well go. Take the day off. Spend some quality time with Lana."

I didn't want to take the day off. I wanted to spend the day here, with him, working out a solution to our myriad problems. But he was right—the election needed to come first, and at the moment, there wasn't anything for me to do. I'd be better off getting my head back in the game before the polls opened tomorrow.

"Right. Good idea." I forced myself to pull back, out of his reach. "Thanks, Daniel. I'll text you later."

With shoes full of lead, I walked away. But I taught myself to dance on a pole with weights attached to my feet, and I could move with shoes full of lead. It was the only way right now.

An impromptu shopping trip might lift my spirits. If nothing else, the mall sold cookie dough and sushi burritos, neither of which could possibly make things any worse. Especially not if I brought my best friend.

Lana met me at her front door with a blender full of mimosas. It was early, but breakfast alcohol is an exception, right? I almost asked for a straw, but accepted the large glass she offered.

Quickly I filled her in on the conversation Daniel and I had that morning. "I'm not even sure I want to be a senator anymore."

"Well, not to piss in your cornflakes, but from what I see on the news, you're not going to be."

Her tone said she teased, but the words hit me in my gut. "That's the whole problem. I decided to run because Curtis wanted to shut down Dance 4 U, and I couldn't stand the thought of losing my livelihood. But from the beginning, Erica insisted that I can't continue to teach even if I win, and Daniel backed her up. Win or lose, I'm out my favorite thing in the world. And now I've lost someone I care about."

Lana scoffed. "If he would let you walk away because of the strain of running for office, he doesn't deserve you."

"That doesn't make me feel any better. I'm losing everything, and it's all completely out of my control," I said. "It's one thing if the voters don't connect with me or my ideas didn't resonate. It's completely different when the one thing that makes people not want to vote for me is what I used to do for a living."

"That's not the only thing. It can't be. What about that guy who was a professional wrestler before he ran for governor? They don't wear a lot of clothes, either, and no one cared."

I sighed and took a long drink. "I agree with you, but apparently that's different. He's got the trifecta: rich, white, male. I am one of those things, and women are historically held to higher standards than men."

"Still, I have to feel like, if the voters truly believe in your message, they'll vote for you."

"That's not what the numbers are showing," I said miserably. "Maybe I should just let Curtis win."

"And then what?" Lana said quietly. "Switch to teaching yoga or spin?"

My head landed on the counter. Into the surface, I mumbled, "I have no idea. Pole is the only thing I've wanted to do for years. I love it. I'm good at it."

"And what about Daniel?"

"We're over," I moaned. "He doesn't like me the way I am."

"I'm not sure that's true. Do you care about each other?"

When we'd been arguing, Daniel said the words, but I hadn't responded. Now he'd never know. I sniffled. "I do. I can't believe I fell so fast, but I did."

"Does he care about you?"

"He says he loves me." The memory made me smile for what felt like the first time in weeks.

"Then don't count yourself out yet. Do you want to be with him, whether you win the election or not?"

I considered her question. When we'd met, I'd liked Daniel instantly. There had been a connection. We chatted easily, I loved bantering with him, and—until our argument after the debate—I felt more centered when he was around. Something about his inner strength and self-possession calmed me. Not to mention that kiss. Oh, man.

Yes, he tried to change me. But he was helping me get the job we both thought I wanted. Right or wrong, I wouldn't have garnered even the sliver of support I got without that help. We both made some bad choices, but I still cared about him.

"You know..." I took a deep breath. "I do. Despite every-thing, he's worth it."

"Then I think you just need some time to clear your head. We'll figure something out, but sitting and staring at your phone isn't the answer. Come on."

Confused, I lifted my head and studied her. "You know I can take my phone with me, right? It's portable."

"Not where we're going."

Her words made me nervous, but I listened with half an ear as I followed her to the car. She chatted about stuff that didn't matter. None of it stayed with me. When we finally pulled into the parking lot of the mall, parking in a space by the movie theater, I laughed. Lana had found the one place I wouldn't use my phone. People who texted—or worse, made calls—in the theater made me want to climb over the seats to yank their devices away. Instead, I turned my phone off and put it into Lana's waiting hand before we got out of the car.

The darkness numbed my brain for the two hours, twenty-seven minutes it took for us to watch the latest teen comedy and roughly fourteen previews. I didn't know what we were watching, but it didn't matter. I ate from a bucket of popcorn as big as my torso and tried not to think.

Unfortunately, that pleasant lack of emotion wore off the second we left the theater and spotted Erica, talking to some guy in a hoodie next to a table in the adjacent food court.

What on earth was she doing here? Was she following me? No, that didn't make any sense.

Lana grabbed the back of my shirt and pulled me behind a post that separated the movie theater from the dining area. I tried to pull away, but she held firm. Silently, I cursed myself for all the hours spent teaching her to improve her grip.

"What are you doing? I don't need to hide from Erica."

"You don't?" Lana dragged me against the wall. I couldn't see Erica but she wouldn't see us, either. "You don't think it's a little weird that she just happened to be here?"

To be honest, the way the campaign was going, I didn't blame Erica for ditching work to hit the mall. Especially not when I'd done the same thing. "I don't know, maybe she's going to a movie. Like everyone else here."

"The woman who has been subtly undermining you every chance she gets—despite being employed to help you— happens to be hanging out at the mall food court the day before the election? Right after you had a huge public melt-down? Why isn't she at campaign headquarters, doing damage control? After all, she still works for you."

"Maybe she's campaigning?" What did it even matter, anymore?

Lana snorted. "No way. She's up to something. For one thing, that guy looks familiar."

My poor friend must be bored out of her mind to be seeing conspiracy theories. "There have to be a thousand guys in the area who wear hoodies. Heck, I'm wearing a hoodie right now."

"True. So am I." Lana pulled her hood up and slipped on her sunglasses, then motioned for me to do the same.

"This is ridiculous," I said but followed her lead.

"Shut up. We're going to see what she's doing. Act natural."

Together, we strolled out of the theater, circling toward the restroom, following the crowd. Erica still stood talking to someone we couldn't see. Lana was right. Something about the man did seem familiar. I pretended to be looking at the poster behind them when the man looked around. Then he reached into his pocket, withdrew a large, flat envelope, and set it on the table while she studied her phone. He walked over to a stand selling subs. A moment later, Erica casually picked up the envelope. She slid it into her purse, eyes still glued to her phone, then walked away without looking at him.

Lana and I continued to track her. Something was wrong about all of this. We needed to know what she was up to.

Erica was short. Very short. Meaning we lost her as she moved among the sea of SUVs in the movie theater parking lot while trying to look casual and not stray too far from Lana's car. There was a reason I'd gone into pole fitness instruction and not P.I. work. Even having been in her car didn't help. It could've been anywhere.

Lana cursed under her breath when we realized we couldn't find Erica anywhere. I started to do the same when the swinging glass doors caught my attention. The guy in the hoodie emerged into the sunlight. Unless we split up, Lana and I couldn't follow both him and Erica, but maybe we could at least figure out who this guy was and why he was secretly passing envelopes to my campaign manager.

"Look! It's him."

"Great. Maybe we can lose *him* in the parking lot, too. We suck at this." She grumbled. "You're too tall. Can't you slouch a little?"

Our quarry turned and walked toward the bus stop. I took off after him, Lana half a step behind. The Capital District wasn't exactly a public transportation hub, so the guy would probably spot us within about four seconds of arriving at the bus stop, but I'd worry about that when it happened. Maybe if I spoke to him, I'd know why he seemed familiar.

The bus pulled to a stop just as we reached the curb. When the guy climbed up the steps, I tried for a peek at hair sticking out of his hoodie, but no luck. Before I could wonder what to do next, Lana hopped on board, so I followed. Shoulders hunched, we stared at the ground and shuffled down the aisle, sitting near the back. Hoodie sat a few rows up, on the left.

The hood of his sweatshirt fell to his shoulders, and I gasped softly. Lana's hand gripped mine, a silent reminder to keep quiet. Or maybe she wanted to stop me from getting out of my seat. I couldn't believe what I was seeing. No wonder the man seemed so familiar. I knew him.

The man sitting not fifteen feet away, the man who'd just had a clandestine meeting with the woman who was slowly making my life as miserable as possible had been on my doorstep not forty-eight hours earlier.

He worked for the Saratoga Dispatch. Jerry Braithwaite. The guy who did my original candidate profile, at Erica's suggestion. The one who approached and snapped pictures of me barely dressed at seven a.m. He posted the old instructional videos, which I'd completely forgotten about. He must be the one who took the pictures of me in the park. Everything that happened, all the public outrage, stemmed from his articles.

Jerry's stories that tanked my numbers in the polls every time I started to pick up some traction. Now I knew why the media didn't follow Curtis around all the time. It wasn't that I was more interesting, like Daniel thought. Jerry had been working with my Communications Director to sabotage my campaign.

# Chapter Twenty-Three

**Cupid:** Sadly, this move neither comes with a bow and arrow nor brings a promise of true love. However, once I finally managed to nail it, I felt like the angels smiled upon me.

*- Push and Pole Fitness Tutorials, Vol. 3*

A shockwave ripped through me at the depth of Erica's betrayal. She knew everything about me, the campaign, our strategy. She looked down on me. That had been obvious from early on. More than once, I'd questioned her politics, but I'd been assured that she worked for the joy of winning (and the love of money), not for either party. I'd never thought she would throw me under the bus. I couldn't believe it.

At least I finally understood why she stuck around. Suddenly, it all made sense: The familiar-looking older woman who Erica had been talking to at the mall. She hadn't been asking for directions to the restroom. Now it seemed clear as day that Erica had been chatting with Mrs. Baker. Whether a planned meeting or just a coincidence, I may never know, but the two of them definitely knew each other.

Erica knew I'd started running in the evenings. She knew there was a playground nearby, and if she'd done any research on polers, she'd know that we loved to hang off things in public. It would've been easy enough to have a reporter follow me. She must've seen me with Daniel at headquarters (and apparently taken a picture). My fingers itched to pick up the phone, make a call, and scream out my rage. But not in public. Especially not with a reporter sitting three feet away.

The bus had only traveled a few blocks since we left the mall. I yanked the cord, silently fuming. Confronting the reporter for doing his job wasn't going to help. The last thing I needed was for tomorrow morning's edition to read "Stripper Politician Attacks Fine, Upstanding Reporter on Bus."

Lana must've agreed, because she was on her feet and at the door before the bus stopped. Neither one of us said a word until we were on the sidewalk.

"Was that…?" she asked.

"Yup."

"Talking to—"

"—that bitch who sold me out? Why, yes, it was. Oh, I can't believe her!"

Fuming, I turned back toward the mall. My legs carried me across the pavement as Lana practically jogged beside me to keep up. I was too furious to speak, and anything she said would've been lost to the wind since she trailed behind me.

Erica. Everything that had gone wrong since the beginning of the campaign was because of my hired image consultant. Now my Communications Director. The woman who was supposed to be helping me. My failing campaign wasn't entirely my fault. The press wouldn't have paid any attention to me without her feeding them dirt. No one except Curtis should've cared what I did for a living. I mean, they all supported an old man who'd thrown away his life's work to sell skincare products out of an RV with a woman young enough to be his granddaughter. "Family values" and "Baker" weren't exactly synonymous, no matter what they wanted people to believe.

When I thought of all the times Erica had looked down her nose at me, all the times she acted so distraught at the media attention, I wanted to punch something. Instead, my rage propelled me forward. A few short minutes later, I arrived back at Lana's car.

I paced until my friend caught up to me. She unlocked the doors but paused before climbing inside. "I assume we're going to Erica's house?"

"You don't have to go with me," I said. "But it's time for the two of us to have a long talk."

My mind raced as Lana drove back to her place so I could pick up my car. I didn't know what to say to Erica, or how to get her to admit what she'd done, but I needed to see her. This couldn't wait.

Less than half an hour later, standing on the front porch of the type of spectacular home I'd never be able to afford, all the wind went out of my sails. No cars in the driveway, no movement behind the curtains. No one responding to the doorbell. If Erica was home, she wasn't opening the door.

Part of me wanted to go in, anyway. Try the windows or walk around the back looking for an unlocked door. But if Erica found out, she'd probably call the police, not to mention Jerry. Daniel would be furious if I got arrested. A burglary charge would be the icing on this craptastic cake of suckitude.

With a heavy sigh, I turned toward the street. I didn't know where to go. I'd foolishly hoped to get a confession from Erica before calling Daniel. He needed to see what a snake she was. I couldn't handle the thought of telling him what I'd seen and having him think I was jumping to conclusions.

As I reached my car, someone said my name. The voice was so quiet, I almost didn't hear it. I swiveled around to find Curtis on the front porch of the house next door, striding toward me. Great. Just what I needed.

What on Earth was he doing here, anyway?

The best defense was a good offense, so I glared at him as if I weren't standing uninvited on Erica's front lawn. "What do you want?"

"Now, now, Ms. Martin, I'm not your enemy."

"Really? Coulda fooled me." I sighed and stuffed my hands in my pockets. "Why are you here?"

"I live here."

My head shot up. "I'm sorry, what?"

He gestured to the large blue two-story home at the end of the sweeping driveway behind him. "This is my parents' home. I grew up here. When my father…er, lost his senses, I moved home to help my mother."

This didn't make any sense. Had I somehow gotten the address wrong? After all, I'd never been to Erica's house before, for obvious reasons. There must be a mistake in the database. Since I still needed to find her, it was time to get the heck out of here. But I couldn't just leave without saying anything. The only thing more awkward than being caught standing outside his house would be bolting the moment he saw me.

"Sorry, I must've written down the wrong address. I was looking for Erica."

"Ah. I suppose that makes sense." He glanced at the still house behind me. "I don't think she's home, though."

Hold up. He couldn't possibly be saying what I thought he was saying. "You and Erica are neighbors?"

"Well, my parents and hers. We grew up together."

Okay, this information changed everything. So many things started to click in my memory. Trying to force myself to focus,

I swallowed and counted to five. "Tell me—how was Erica's relationship with your mother before she moved?"

"Two peas in a pod," he said. "Mom wrote the recommendation to get Erica into Boston College. Why do you ask?"

The final puzzle piece fell into place. Erica's disdain wasn't about me. She was here to help Mrs. Baker restore the family image. And I was the naive fool who didn't do enough research, didn't ask nearly enough questions about any of the people working for me.

Time to go. If she wasn't home, confronting her wouldn't work. This whole conversation took a lot of the wind out of my sails. I needed to regroup, talk to Daniel, decide on a plan of action. See if there was anything left to salvage.

Another thought stopped me cold in my tracks: what if he knew? Daniel and Erica were old friends. Daniel had known Curtis for decades. Erica had known Curtis for decades. They were next-door neighbors, for god's sake. And Daniel hired her.

No.

I had to believe he wasn't part of this. Because if Daniel knew about Erica's treachery, then everything he claimed to feel for me had been a lie. My poor heart couldn't take that. Even if we couldn't be together, I couldn't believe that I'd had feelings for such a snake. Still, I needed to talk to him, immediately.

Before I left, though, there was something I had to know. "Curtis, can I ask you a question?"

He shrugged. "Sure."

"Why are you doing this? Daniel told me about you, and the person he described didn't care about pole or even stripping or any of this. Heck, he's suggested that there may be a photo or two of you cozying up to a man on a pole out there somewhere."

All the color drained from his face. "Hold on… are you blackmailing me?"

I sighed. "No. That's the difference between you and me. I don't want to win that way. I don't care that you're gay. I don't want anyone who does to use your personal business as a reason to vote for me instead of you. Or not to vote at all."

He suddenly turned ramrod straight, glancing at the house over his shoulder. Probably worried that Mommy Dearest would hear me spilling his deepest secret. "I'm sorry, but I'm afraid I'm going to have to ask you to leave."

"Sure. Whatever." Coming here had been a waste of time, and trying to connect with Curtis as a human being made me feel like an idiot.

I got in the car, letting the door slam. My phone pulled up directions to campaign headquarters, so I shifted the car into gear. At the corner, I allowed myself to glance back, looking once more for any signs of life at Erica's house.

Instead I saw Curtis, still standing on the sidewalk, watching me go.

# Chapter Twenty-Four

**Chopper:** This move looks impressive, but once you've built up your core strength, it's fairly simple. With a bit of practice, soon you'll find yourself able to hang upside-down from almost anything.

*- Push and Pole Fitness Tutorials, Vol. 3*

When I got to campaign headquarters, Daniel was on a call, so I started texting my old students, setting up lessons again. Erica was the one who'd insisted I stop giving teaching any one-on-one sessions, that I take down the pole in my condo until after the election. Her opinion meant nothing now, not when she'd been secretly working against me the whole time. Without her constantly calling the media on me, no one would be peeking into my windows, even if I won.

And if they did, well, I had curtains. Also the ability to call the police on them for trespassing. I was done giving up all the things I loved. Erica ruined my chances of winning the election, nipped my relationship with Daniel in the bud, took away all my hobbies—no more. Pole exhilarated me. The thrill of nailing a new move, the look of wonder when a student accomplished something she'd thought impossible. I wanted that back.

One by one, I explained to my best students that I planned to get back to teaching immediately. Even though the old space may not be available until after the hearing, I was looking for a new location. I offered to set up discounted private appointments for the following week. Although the press crucified me every chance they got, my students loved me. They just wanted to get strong, learn cool tricks, and awe their friends and family. Time to make some money and take my mind off everything that happened since I made that stupid live stream.

By the time Daniel finished his call, I'd scheduled five lessons for the next day. Might as well keep busy until the polls closed and the results started rolling in. It only took a few minutes to fill him in on the things Lana and I discovered.

When I finished, he simply sat there, shaking his head. "I can't believe it. Erica has always been so good at keeping her personal and private life separate."

"Did you know that she and Curtis are neighbors?"

"No. It never would've occurred to me to ask where she lived." He tapped on his keyboard for a few minutes, then stopped to read something. "Here it is. Erica inherited that property when her mother died last year. That's around the time she returned from D.C."

I sighed. "I still don't get why she would do any of this. She took the job to hurt me—why? Because I happened to be running against her former neighbor? Because she and Curtis's mom used to be close? She could've just turned us down. There was no reason to sabotage the campaign."

Daniel's eyes continued to travel down the computer screen, skimming the page as I spoke. He clicked a couple of times, then the blood drained from his face. "I can't believe I missed this."

"What?"

Instead of answering, he turned the screen. He'd somehow accessed a document filed with the D.C. family court. I leaned forward and devoured the words. A little over a year ago, Erica Popov of Washington, D.C. filed for divorce from her husband, Doug Popov, claiming irreconcilable differences—and adultery. My eyes tripped over one of the allegations.

"Her ex-husband left her for a stripper?" With each word, my voice grew higher. "Her ex-husband left her for a stripper *and you hired her to help a pole fitness teacher win a state election?*"

"I'm so sorry, Melody." He hung his head in his hands before going back to the screen. When he spoke again, disbelief filled his voice. "According to this, her husband also took their savings and saddled her with a significant amount of debt."

Closing my eyes, I shook my head. "I can't believe this."

"I swear, I had no idea. I've known Erica for years. She's a great strategical thinker, with a sharp political mindset. We're old friends. When she moved back to the area, I thought she was a godsend."

"Well, someone sent her, but I don't think God had much to do with it," I said bitterly.

He sighed. "I don't believe it."

"You swear you didn't know about this?"

"I swear," he said, his eyes earnest. "Our relationship has always been surface level. We were acquaintances, then colleagues. I didn't ask why her marriage failed. We were never close, and to be honest, it never occurred to me."

With a heavy sigh, I leaned back in my chair. "So what do we do now?"

Behind me, a bell rang to indicate that someone had come in the front door. In my haste to get to Daniel and tell him about Erica's betrayal, I must've forgotten to lock it behind me. Unless it was someone with a key.

A shared glance told me that he'd had the same thought. Together, we left the office to greet our new arrival.

It wasn't Erica. To my surprise and dismay, the second-to-last person I wanted to see ever again stood in our doorway. Probably coming to gloat. What a day.

"Why didn't we hire a security guard?" I muttered, just loud enough for him to hear.

"Hey, Melody. I need to talk to Daniel for a minute," Curtis said.

"I hope you don't think you can get us to drop out."

"That's not why I'm here, but by all means, feel free."

My campaign manager chuckled and shook his head. "It's not going to be that easy. You'll need to get votes the old fashioned way. Your platform is abominable, so you'll need to rely on your charm and charisma."

I snorted.

"Funny you should mention that," he said. "I've been thinking my platform could use a few tweaks."

"Oh, yeah? You want to stop gays from adopting now? Forced pregnancy for women of child-bearing age?" Daniel asked.

He chuckled. "I love sparring with you. We really should work together again at some point. And no, that's not what I mean at all. I assume Melody told you about our earlier conversation?"

"She did. Why?"

"There's something I need to tell you."

Daniel glanced at the big storefront windows facing out onto the street. The road shouldn't be busy this time of day, but anyone who happened to wander by would see us. As would Erica if she appeared. I didn't expect her to drop by, but she didn't know that she'd been discovered.

"Are we okay here?" I asked.

"Let's go back to my office."

We sat again, this time with me pulling up a chair beside Daniel behind the desk. Two on one. Once everyone got settled, I leaned forward and put my elbows on the desk. "Okay. What do you have to say that's so important?"

Curtis held up an envelope similar to the one the reporter gave Erica. I raised my eyebrows at him but said nothing. He took a deep breath. "Some information has come to my attention. I consider it my duty to tell you—as you know, we agreed to a clean campaign. The two of you deserve to have all the facts. I never wanted to win like this."

"Are you saying you and Erica weren't working together?"

He shook his head. "Not at all. I was trying to repair my family's image after my father abandoned his post. When I decided to run, the last thing I wanted was to take the campaign in a personal direction. I had as much to lose as you did."

"I never would have outed you to win," I said.

"I know," he said. "I realized that the night you met Mom. And I was wrong to use your past against you. I'm afraid I let her views influence me too much. She was so depressed when Dad left, a completely different person. When I told her I wanted to run for his seat, it invigorated her. She came back to life. I allowed myself to take her ideas and run with them."

"Why are you telling me all this?" As much as interfamily dynamics fascinated me, I didn't understand what Curtis was doing at my campaign headquarters if he hadn't come to gloat.

"Because I wasn't the only one influenced by my mother. She's been spending a lot of time with Erica. And now I understand why." He cleared his throat. "A couple of minutes after you left, Erica zoomed into her garage. She went out the back door and came over to our yard."

"She just wanders into your back yard any time she

wants?" Maybe Curtis was the one who should get a dog. I wondered if Princess Sofia Sassypants still needed a new home. Although she may not be the best watchdog unless a burglar was terrified of being snuggled to death.

Curtis shrugged. "We grew up together. We've had that adjoining fence since we were kids. Anyway, I tried to get close enough to listen, hear what she and Mom were talking about, but they clammed up whenever I got within ten feet. I took them a bottle of wine, then snuck out and headed over to Erica's house."

Wow. I couldn't believe what he was telling us. Somehow, I'd inspired my opponent to commit a felony for me. This wasn't the Curtis I'd gotten to know over the past few weeks, but my respect for him was rising steadily.

"You took a big risk," Daniel said. "What if she'd caught you?"

"I needed to see what was going on. I knew the back door was unlocked," he said. "Inside her office, a phone flashed on the desk. It wasn't her regular smartphone."

From his pocket, he produced a small blue flip phone, the type I hadn't seen in ages. I resisted the urge to reach for it. "Do those things still work?"

Daniel snorted. "Apparently, so. But, Curtis, why did you bring us an old phone?"

"That's the thing. It's not an old phone." Triumph laced his voice. "There are only two phone numbers in the call history. The first one is the number for our house. Same landline we've had for decades. The other I googled. It belongs to Jerry Braithwaite at the Albany Times."

The guy from the mall. No shocker there, all things considered. If Curtis expected my expression to register surprise, he was disappointed. Too weary from it all to speak, I nodded.

"You knew?"

"Saw them together about an hour ago. That's why I

stopped by Erica's house in the first place. I wanted to confront her."

"They're not just talking," Curtis said. "Once I put the phone away, I spotted these sitting on her desk."

He offered the envelope to me, and I took it gingerly, still not quite believing what was happening.

The envelope contained several pictures of me, some taken through my condo windows. Darn it, I really needed to use my curtains. None of the pictures were terribly interesting, though. Probably because I hadn't done much in the past few days. But then Curtis handed me a bank statement with Erica's name at the top. The balance was zero, and there were almost no transactions. Halfway down the page, I spotted a cash deposit for five thousand dollars, which was immediately transferred to an account at another bank. A second deposit appeared below it. Both were made at a bank branch a couple of blocks from the Baker home.

My heart leaped into my throat. Suddenly, it all made sense. Erica's husband left her for a stripper. He took everything with him. She associated pole fitness with stripping, and therefore assumed I was no better than the woman who'd "stolen" her husband. She'd always been conservative—Daniel told me, ages ago, that his college roommate dumped her for saving herself for marriage. Curtis's mother was religious. The two of them knew each other well.

Mr. Baker used to represent the family in the state senate. He resigned in a manner that left them open to ridicule. Now that Curtis was running, Mrs. Baker couldn't stand the thought of him losing to someone with "loose morals." She'd been paying Erica to help Curtis win this whole time.

Mouth open, I turned to Daniel. He looked as shell-shocked as I felt. For a long moment, neither of us could speak. Finally, he looked across the desk. "I assume that, in light of all of this information, you're planning to drop out and concede the election?"

He nodded, looking miserable. "It's the right thing to do. As much as I loved working with my father, loved being in politics, I can't take the job knowing that my mother conspired to sabotage my opponent. That's completely unacceptable."

Finally, I found my voice. "No."

They both turned to me, identically confused faces.

"You're not dropping out, Curtis. I am."

# Chapter Twenty-Five

**The Attitude:** An excellent spin for when you're feeling sassy. Grasp the pole with your dominant arm above your head and walk in a circle. Bring your other arm across your belly to grasp the pole, creating a triangle with the pole. The top arm provides your push, the bottom arm your pull. Hook your front leg on the pole, and push off with your back leg, lifting it behind you and giving you momentum to spin.

*- Push and Pole Fitness Tutorials, Vol. 1*

"You said it yourself. You love politics. You loved working with your father. You love verbal sparring. I don't. I don't love any of it. All I ever wanted was to teach pole fitness."

"Then why did you run for office?" Curtis asked. "Why not support another candidate?"

"Because you got an injunction against me! I couldn't work, and I was pissed." In retrospect, perhaps running for state senate out of spite wasn't the best decision ever. Although it should've been fine. If Erica hadn't been plotting against me, I might have won. Early on, the voters responded to me. They found me fresh and interesting.

His face turned red. "Right. That was Mom's idea. Sorry about that."

Fat lot of good it did me now. "I only ran because you said you were going to shut me down permanently if you won. As soon as Erica told me I wouldn't be able to work as a legislator and be a dance teacher, I knew I'd made a mistake. But it was too late to pull out."

"It's never too late," Curtis said. "And you can't stop me from dropping out. I don't want to win because my mother smeared you in the press. It's not right. I'll find another job, maybe run for Assembly in the fall. Or even take some time off, figure out what I really want. I've got the money Dad gave me before he took off."

"Yeah, well, you can't stop me, either!" I glared at him defiantly.

"Hold on," Daniel said. "So neither of you wants to fill Tiberius's seat?"

We both shook our heads, equal looks of determination. Daniel looked like he wasn't sure if he wanted to laugh or cry. Leaning back against the desk, he stared at the wall for a long time. "Okay, then. What do we do now?"

"I've been thinking about that a lot," I said. "I don't have the right look for politics. I don't have the right personality, background, or experience. Sure, I can learn about the law and procedure, but shouldn't we vote for someone who already knows about these things?"

"I already told you, there's no way I'm doing it," Daniel said. "Not to mention, it's too late to move into the district."

"I know, I know," I said. "But listen up. I have an idea."

By the time I finished explaining, Daniel was nodding

along with me. "Somehow, I had a feeling you were going to say that."

"It's perfect, right?"

"Perfect is not the word I would use to describe any of this," Daniel said. "But I suppose it makes sense, in light of everything that's happened."

Curtis shrugged. "You've certainly got balls, Melody."

"Thanks," I said. "Do we have a deal?"

"Yeah. I'm going back to my office. I need to call a press conference. For this to work, I should go first."

Daniel said, "We'll wait twenty minutes, then do the same. Good luck."

It didn't take long to drive home. My mind raced, turning the day's events over and over. As badly as I'd wanted to confront Erica, this was even better. She'd be completely caught off-guard by our double announcements, and she'd be pissed that she had to find out secondhand from the news.

Not from her good friend Jerry, though. He wasn't invited to the conferences. Erica and Jerry could read about our agreement on social media, like everyone else.

Lana met me and Daniel at my front door, carrying her pole in a bag on her shoulder. Portable poles also adjusted to almost any ceiling height. Soon enough, I'd take my pole back from Erica. She had no right to keep it. But for today, I appreciated my best friend bringing me both the physical and emotional support.

"Thank you so much for coming."

"You've got this," she said. "You're doing something extremely brave, you know."

"Not extremely stupid?"

"Sometimes the right thing is both," Daniel said. "I admit, I don't think this is going to work."

"Shush. It's never stupid to stand up for yourself. You've got this." Lana wrapped her arms tightly around me, then pivoted and pushed me toward my bedroom. "Daniel and I will set up. Go. Get ready."

A long shower erased much of the tension from my shoulders. Having made a decision left me feeling a thousand times better. I took great care in getting dressed, pulling out my highest heels, my most glittery bra top, and the black booty shorts that always left me strutting with confidence.

Daniel waited for me in the living room, along with the members of the media who had been able to show up at the last minute. We got more than I expected. He grinned when he saw me. The admiration on his face made me feel even better about what I was doing.

Eyes widened when I entered the room. A smirk played across my lips. They all thought they knew what I was going to say. I gazed back, head held high. The time for pretending to be someone else passed. Before all this started, I'd never been ashamed to be myself. It had been wrong to let Erica destroy my sense of self. Lana had been right all along, but I'd been too afraid to listen to her.

"Thank you, everyone, for coming," I said to the reporters packed into my small entryway. "I know it was last minute for you. Over the past several weeks, I've been getting a lot of media attention. I guess I shouldn't have been surprised since I am running for public office. But the weird thing to me was that no one seemed to care about the issues. Instead, people seemed awfully concerned about the fact that I like to dance on a pole. It's just an apparatus, like a balance beam. But to some people, doing pole makes me some kind of 'loose woman.'"

In the audience, someone snorted. I stifled a laugh.

"That gem came directly from the mouth of my opponent's mother. Thanks, Mrs. Baker, but I'm not a sex worker. And if I were, I'd still be worthy of respect as a human being."

A couple more flashbulbs hit me in the face. One reporter raised a hand, followed by another, until everyone seemed to have something to ask. Daniel asked them all to hold their questions until the end, and the hands slowly went down.

I continued my prepared speech. "If I can't win this election without abandoning my sense of self, then I haven't won at all. I refuse to continue pretending to be someone else. I'm proud of what I've accomplished. I love what I do, and I'm sorry I ever thought I needed to live a lie to get elected.

"From the day I entered this campaign, people have come after me: I've been called a sex worker, a stripper, a slut. This isn't just insulting, it's lazy reporting. I can't believe that you all have nothing better to do than slut-shame me for my perceived choices. How can we live in a society that condemns women for working as strippers, as sex workers, without also condemning the men that provide a constant demand for these services? What we should be talking about is passing laws that protect any woman who needs it. People shouldn't be demonizing me for doing what I love. From day one, I haven't heard anyone raise a single question about Curtis Baker's morality. Now, I'm not here to do that, either, because it's irrelevant. What's relevant is the way the media focuses on his ideas and my morality. This is an unacceptable double standard. And if the people of Saratoga are okay with it, I'm very sorry to say, I don't want to represent you."

My voice started to shake, so I stopped and forced myself to count to five. This was the right thing to do. As much as it felt good to take a stand, I'd been miserable since the minute this campaign started. Working in the state legislature wouldn't improve things, not if I couldn't be me while I did it.

"It is my understanding that, within the past hour, Mr. Baker has withdrawn from the election. He told you that I would also be speaking, and asked you to listen to what I have to say with an open mind. I'd like to thank Mr. Baker, and let him know that I bear no ill will toward him for what happened. He isn't responsible for the way the campaign got ugly. I recently discovered that my own image consultant, Erica Wentworth, was working with a reporter to sabotage me."

Someone in the crowd gasped. Heads turned, probably looking to see who hadn't been invited to the conference. A few hands shot up, but I ignored them.

"No, I'm not going to tell you who it was. It doesn't matter. However, it turns out—I'm just not cut out for politics. This isn't what I want to do, and I don't like the person it's turning me into. And that is why I asked you here. To announce that I've also decided to terminate my campaign for the New York Senate. If I have to pretend to be someone I'm not to get your votes, the cost is too high."

Someone gasped. In the front row, a woman nodded along as I spoke. Someone started clapping. Soon another person followed suit. Before I knew it, the crowd rose to their feet, giving me a standing ovation. Someone that sounded suspiciously like Daniel whistled.

On the other side of my makeshift podium, cameras clicked and flashed away. I beamed, soaking it all in.

"Now, there's someone else I'd like to tell you about. Someone who has held my hand throughout this campaign. Who has helped me mold myself into a person that the people of this district would be lucky to have represent them. Who has taught me the law and the unspoken practices of the area. Someone brilliant, talented, and full of fresh ideas. She's exactly what this district needs to help get our voice heard at the statehouse. That person is local attorney and campaign advisor Lana Chen." I gestured to my best friend in the back of the room as I spelled her name.

She waved to the room, face beet red, but said nothing. She didn't think for a minute that anyone was going to vote for her, except me and Daniel. But she'd be brilliant in the job, as long as she believed in herself.

"Please consider writing Lana Chen onto the ballot when you go to vote tomorrow."

The room fell silent. Everyone either scribbled furiously in notebooks, tapped away at their phones, or stared at me blankly. Pretty much the reaction I'd expected. After all, who was I to ask them to vote for some random person?

I threw my head back. Mel Martin, that's who. Kick-ass dancer, excellent teacher, and newly prepared to share my opinion with everyone who needed to hear it. "Anyway, now that I've got your attention—Who'd like a pole demonstration?"

Every hand in the room shot into the air, including Daniel's and Lana's.

Fifteen minutes later, one reporter after another thanked me as they filed out of the small room. They'd been completely awed by my moves, and several even promised to sign up for classes once I got my new studio up and running. Finally, things were starting to look up.

Eventually only Lana and Daniel hung back. My BFF caught the glance I gave her and disappeared into the bathroom.

"Working with you has certainly been an experience." Daniel picked up his coat from where he'd slung it on the kitchen island and spent a long time smoothing it over his arm. He put it on, before taking it off and folding it over his arm a second time. Then he cleared his throat. "You know, I never thought one of my candidates would teach me how to twirl on a metal bar."

"I'm always here if you want a refresher." My head tilted toward the pole. There were so many other things I wanted to say, but it was too late. There was no point. The election was over, I was going back to my old self, and Mel and Daniel didn't fit. Maybe Melody and Daniel never fit, either.

He winced. "My muscles are still sore from the last time. Anyway, thank you for trying."

"Are you going to work with Lana if she actually gets elected?" I wasn't sure what answer I wanted. Yes, Lana would probably benefit from his knowledge and experience. But knowing she got to see him every day when I couldn't might kill me.

He considered the question for a long moment. "If she'll have me. After all, she might think I helped throw her to the wolves."

"To be fair, you did," she said, returning from the bathroom. I'd almost forgotten that she was still here, but she needed to remove her pole before she left. Hopefully quickly. "But I sincerely doubt it'll matter."

"Don't count yourself out," I said. "There were plenty of people in this room who want that seat filled."

"They'll probably all write their own names in," she said, carefully arranging the metal pieces in her purple striped bag before zipping it closed. "Anyway, this was a blast. Text me later?"

"I'll give you a call if anyone other than Mel and I vote for you." Daniel made no movement to follow her to the door. We stood side-by-side, arms almost touching. I prayed no one would do or say anything that might make him decide to go rather than stay back with me. If this was going to be the last time I saw him, I needed more.

"In that case, I won't hold my breath." She blew air kisses at both of us, slung the pole bag over her shoulder, and headed out.

"You know, in a special election, two write-in votes might be enough," I reminded Daniel as soon as the door shut behind her. "You were the one concerned about low voter turnout."

"Touché. But I also think it's better not to stress Lana out until we see what happens. Listen, I'm doing some research on legislation for the next year or so. New laws to further protect free expression, women's rights, that kind of thing. Equal pay."

My ears perked up. "Oh, yeah?"

"Yeah. Someone convinced me that we've still got a long way to go before our state achieves equality."

His words brought a smile to my face. He really did care about other people. "You're a good man, Daniel O'Brien."

For a long moment I gazed at him, still somewhat bemused by the day's events. At eight o'clock this morning, I'd been wallowing in self-pity, running a losing campaign, with no job prospects for after I lost. Now I had my studio, an unexpected alliance, and a level of personal satisfaction that had been noticeably absent since the night Curtis shut Dance 4 U down. Not bad for a day's work.

Only one thing was missing. My hand itched to reach up, smooth back those gorgeous red locks, touch his cheek, but there was no point. We were from different worlds. This needed to be good-bye. Maybe I'd see him around Lana's office once in a while.

He cleared his throat. "There's something else before I go."

"Oh, yeah?" I forced myself to keep my tone light.

"I made a huge mistake, Mel." His use of my nickname was music to my ears. He hadn't said it since the day I met Erica.

My breath hitched. "You mean, you made a huge mistake when allowing me to drop out and ask everyone to vote for Lana?"

"No." He stepped closer, looking down at me with serious eyes. My heart stuttered at his nearness. "I made a huge mistake in not doing everything in my power to be with you. In asking you to change, making you feel like you weren't good enough the way you were. In walking away from you after the debate instead of begging you to give me another chance."

I'd dreamed of those words for so long, I couldn't quite believe I was hearing them. "Hold on. Are you saying—?"

"I want to be with you."

My heart lifted, but part of me wasn't sure I trusted him after everything that happened. "How? Why? I mean…what changed?"

"You were right. Everything you said. I got so focused on winning that I didn't see how much of you was getting lost in the process. Maybe because you felt free to be yourself around me, I don't know. But it's been a pleasure to get to know the real Mel—and I don't want to let her go."

"How do I know you won't try to change me again? I'm not the perfect politician, and I'm not even the perfect political pundit's partner." Try saying that one five times fast.

His gaze remained steady. "You are the perfect Mel Martin, and that is all I ever want you to be."

My remaining doubts fled. A giddy laugh escaped me, a sound of pure joy that rang through the condo. I threw my arms around his neck, savoring the feel of his body against mine.

"I've missed that sound," Daniel said.

"I've missed you," I replied.

"I'm so sorry," Daniel said. "I never should have tried to change you."

"I'm sorry I let you. I should have had more faith in myself."

"You're amazing, just the way you are. And you're exactly the person I want to be with. You're messy where I'm organized, passionate where I'm cool and collected, daring where I'm reserved." He took a deep breath. "You're the push to my pull."

I laughed. "You mean some of that 'mumbo jumbo' from our lesson sank in?"

"I ate up every word." His lips found mine.

I met him eagerly, desperate to drink him in. My hands moved from his neck to his chin, running over his so-sexy stubble before cupping his face so I could savor the moment. I could have stood there all day, locked against him.

"You're an amazing woman, exactly the way you are. Never forget that again."

I kissed him again, lightly. "If I do, you'll be right here to remind me."

"Count on it."

# Epilogue

**SARATOGA DISPATCH ONLINE**

## WRITE-IN CANDIDATE WINS HOTLY CONTESTED SENATE RACE

The results of Tuesday's special election are in! After working in Tiberius Baker's office for years, candidate Curtis Baker expected to sail into the open seat when his father retired. However, those dreams dissipated when Senator Baker stood up in the middle of a floor debate on teachers' pay, announced that he had been called "to do greater things," and walked out. The shocking move led some to speculate over the value of the Baker name. Many residents felt it was time for someone new to step in.

Enter Melody Martin. She's young, she's brash, she reminds people of Alexandria Ocasio-Cortez—a comparison that makes Martin beam. But she also has an image problem, as a full-time pole fitness instructor. Many district residents seemed biased against a female candidate who shows so much skin for a living.

On Monday, less than 12 hours before the polls opened, each candidate held a press conference. Baker admitted that most of the negative press directed at Martin originated with his mother, apologized profusely, and withdrew from the election. Martin was expected to respond to this announcement. Instead, she railed at anyone who engaged in slut-shaming, and announced that she also was dropping out of the election. (See full story.) She asked voters to write in the name of Lana Chen, a local attorney who has worked on the Martin campaign as an advisor for the past several weeks.

After both candidates announced their refusal to take the office after all, and with nothing else on the ballot, turnout dropped to unprecedented (but not exactly surprising) numbers. When all was said and done, the leading vote-getter was…Lana Chen, who received fifteen write-in votes. Senator-Elect Chen did not immediately return a call for comment. We'll be posting updates as more information about her identity comes to light.

(Click here to receive text alerts.)

**You Might Also Enjoy:**
**SYTYCD, Ms. Martin?**
**How does the Write-in Vote Work?**

# Acknowledgments

First and foremost, thank you to my amazing editor Jami Nord. This book is about forty thousand times better since you've read it. :- ) Thanks to Kirsty McManus for this beautiful cover and Morgan Wright for animating it for me.

Thank you to everyone who entered my contest to name Princess Sofia Sassypants, especially my winner, Lisa Pierce. Thank you Kerry for spending a morning discussing local politics and senate districts with me. I hope we can make it to the track soon.

Always and forever, thank you to my amazing husband for believing in me. And thank you to my readers for your support.

I hope you enjoyed this book. If so, please consider leaving an honest review on **Bookbub** or with your favorite retailer.

What's it like to find yourself elected to local office when you weren't even running?

Read on for a sneak peek at THE ACCIDENTAL SENATOR, Push and Pole Book 2

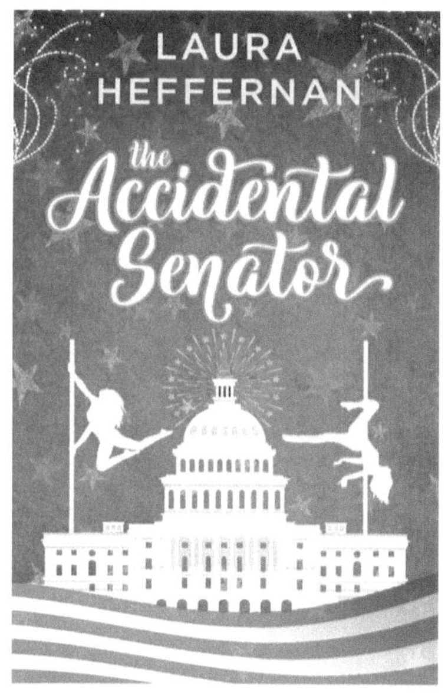



~

## CHAPTER 1

Fifteen votes. Fifteen forking votes (Sorry, I'm trying to curb the swearing now that I'm a *State Senator*). I wasn't even running. No one's ever won with the write-in vote, have they? Note to self: Google "write-in wins" later.

Never thought I'd be a trendsetter. Neither did anyone else, which is why I'd been voted "Least Likely to be a Trendsetter" in high school.

All this ran through my head on repeat as I hurried up the steps to front door of the public building and went through the metal detectors. Once I reclaimed my purse from the conveyor belt, I looked around, desperately trying to figure out where to go for my first day of work. There's no massive orientation following a special election the way there would be in January, so I arrived to quiet halls and hushed voices and an email telling me to look for my mentor. Hopefully I'd figure things out.

Like where the hashtag to find my office. Ever since I arrived at the massive building that housed the state legislative offices, I'd been wandering up and down, listening to my heels clack along the floor, echoing down the halls. Although it was fairly early on the morning, I hadn't seen another soul, making me either embarrassingly late on my first day or that dork who always showed up too early.

For the third time, I consulted my phone. Jason Park, that was the person assigned to show me around. Now only if I could find—oof!

Something slammed into me. My phone hit the floor and skittered across the tile. Looking up, I found myself staring into a gorgeous pair of brown eyes, framed with thick, lush black lashes. The owner of the eyes was taller than me, but not too tall, with short, spiky black hair and perfect lips. He looked muscular but not too buff. Strong and solid.

"I'm so sorry," he said. "Are you Lana Chen?"

"What gave me away?"

"The name on your pass." He pointed.

Oh, right. I'd hung my ID card around my neck for lack of any better place to put it. On my first day, chances were I'd be showing the thing about four dozen times.

I grinned at him. "It labels me a newbie?"

"Nah, just makes you easy to spot." He held out one hand. "I'm Jason."

"Ah, yes! You're the Asian Welcome Wagon?"

His lips twitched. "Yes, of course. And you're the stripper?"

"Touché," I said. "It's nice to meet you."

Jason turned around and led me down the hall to my office, pointing out various points of interest along the way. "I'm actually the liaison for all new Senate Staff."

"Good to know. I left my pasties at home." They'd been worn when Mel needed me to help out at a presentation, over other clothes, but whatevs.

He chuckled. "It's good that you have a sense of humor. That'll serve you well around here."

"I figured I could either make jokes or spend the day lecturing people about misogyny in the world and the dangers of slut-shaming," I said. "I don't like to lecture before I've finished my coffee."

Redness tinged his cheeks, as if I'd touched on a nerve. Good. If I accomplished nothing else before the end of my term, I would get people to stop making women feel bad for using their bodies to find work. Whether it was because they had no other choice or because they enjoyed it.

"Here we are!" Jason turned the corner and opened a door on the right side of the hallway. It stuck. He pushed again, and the door opened a couple of inches. "Sorry. We may need to call Maintenance. Something's wrong."

"Let me try." I waved him back and examined the door. I might be short, but I was strong. Resting my shoulder against the door, I gave it a good shove.

The door flew open. Something on the other side crashed. I stumbled into the room. It took a few steps before I caught my balance, thanks largely to a mountain of cardboard blocking the path.

"What the fork?"

Large boxes packed the room reserved for my administrative assistant from one end to the next, in places stacked three or four high. I couldn't even see the door to my own office, which theoretically was somewhere on the far wall. Words stamped on the outside of each box identified the contents as belonging to a popular line of skin care products. That couldn't be right. But then I remembered. The reason I wound up here in the first place was that my predecessor had a "revelation" of some sort. He invested heavily in a multi-level marketing scheme, selling products from an RV, and resigned.

Jason stepped into the space behind me, glancing around. "Uh…it appears that Senator Baker may have left a few things behind."

Awesome. There wasn't even a way to get to the inner office, where I'd be working. My assistant's desk was completely buried. This wasn't going to work. All that junk needed to go, ASAP. I didn't have a way to contact the former Senator, but I did have the number for his son, Curtis. We'd gotten to know each other over the past couple of months, although it might be a stretch to call us friends.

Texting wouldn't do this thing justice, so I pulled up a video chat and flipped the camera around to show the office.

"Why are you calling me from a warehouse?" Curtis asked. For the first time since we'd met, he was dressed casually in jeans and a t-shirt, dark hair tousled. He looked fresh and well-rested, as if unemployment agreed with him.

"Good question," I asked. "Did you by any chance know where your father was storing all the garbage he bought for his MLM?"

The color drained from Curtis's face as realization dawned. "He didn't."

"I'm afraid he did."

"So sorry, Lana," he said. "I'll talk to him. For now, call Scott in maintenance and ask if they'll put everything in storage for a few days. Let them know I'll take care of it as soon as I can."

As his father's former Chief of Staff, Curtis knew everything about this building and the people who worked in it. Too bad I couldn't ask him to show me around on my first day, since I wouldn't be here if he'd won the election. We'd become friendly, but not that friendly.

It took most of the morning to clean out my new space. The maintenance staff came to help, but even with two dollies at our disposal, it took some time. Turned out, the boxes extended beyond the welcome area into my office. Regular pole fitness classes kept me strong, but my pencil skirt wasn't exactly designed for bending and lifting.

When we finished, Jason took a satisfied look around the inner office. "Much better! You have a reception desk! With phone and a computer. Even a chair. See how well we treat our newest senators?"

"Wow. I sure hope all this special treatment doesn't go to my head. All this, and my own personal senator to show me around."

"Well, that would be lovely, but I'm afraid I have to go soon," Jason said. "We'll talk more later, but one of the first things you should do is hire a Chief of Staff."

"Yeah, I have an idea about that, but if you have any recommendations, I'd appreciate it." Daniel O'Brien, the man who'd run my best friend's campaign and her boyfriend, would probably step in and manage my staff for me if I asked him to. We'd had a couple of conversations about it. But since I was officially only filling in as State Senator until this term ended in January, he felt like he'd be more useful running my re-election campaign.

We only had a few months to convince people that the write-in candidate who'd gotten a whopping fifteen votes should get a chance to serve a full term. Assuming that I wanted to stick around.

"I'll have my Chief of Staff email you later," he said. "I'm sure he can make some suggestions. You'll also need an assistant."

That, at least, was no problem. My current assistant had been with me since I started at the law firm a few years earlier. She'd become a surrogate mother, and I wouldn't even consider moving into a new position without her. She was spending the day packing up my old files and transferring them to the associate who'd be taking over all my cases. "Nancy will be here tomorrow."

"Okay, great. Looks like you're on top of things," Jason said. "I've got a meeting, but IT should be here soon to get you set up in the system. Meanwhile, I brought some forms for you to fill out. Payroll and other HR stuff. If you need anything, please don't hesitate to reach out. I'll be back to take you to the cafeteria for lunch."

He'd helped me so much already, my first instinct was to point out that I could follow my nose to the cafeteria. It would be nice to eat with a friendly face, though. The thought of eating alone in a sea of strangers took me back to elementary school. My dad was in the military, so we moved around a lot. I hated being the new kid. When Dad took early retirement and settled in Albany the summer before my junior year, it was the happiest day of my life.

"Thanks." I watched him go with a small pang and turned my attention to the mountain of paperwork that already needed my attention. As a lawyer, I couldn't even fill out the W-9 or the Direct Deposit authorization forms without reading every word, so it might take a while.

I couldn't believe how far in over my head I'd found myself. My first instinct was to call Mel and ask her what the Horatio she'd been thinking, asking people to write in my name on the ballot. I'd only been a lawyer for a few years. As much as I appreciated my best friend's faith in me, and the idea of being in a position to make a difference excited me a lot more than defending worker's compensation claims, I was terrified.

What if I failed spectacularly? What if I wound up as much as a punchline as the man who'd occupied this office before me?

Moments after his footsteps receded down the hall, my door slammed open, bouncing off the wall. I leapt to my feet as a tall woman with long, swishy red hair stormed into my space. "I need to see Senator Baker immediately."

Jason was right. I definitely needed an assistant.

Buy now to keep reading!

# Get a free novella!

Did you like this book? Sign up for my newsletter at www.lauraheffernan.com and get a **FREE** copy of *Time of My Life*, my gender-flipped Dirty Dancing reboot. Just a little gift from me to you.

**She's a poor dance teacher. He's her rich student. If they can overcome their differences, this could be love.**

Legend says everyone who boards the Oceanic Aphrodite finds love. Janey's on the ship to teach pole fitness, not for romance. Then she meets Frank. He's everything Janey isn't—refined, classy, rich—but his good looks and charm make him undeniably appealing. Unfortunately, he's also a passenger.

When Janey's partner can't perform in the end-of-cruise talent show, Frank offers to fill in. He's never done pole, so he's got to learn fast. As they grow closer, Janey finds herself hoping the legend is real—but if she gives in to temptation, she could be out of a job.

SIGN UP FOR MY MAILING LIST TO GET YOUR FREE COPY.

*Right, left, up, swing left leg around, climb, fall backward, pause.* The steps for my doubles routine went through my head on repeat while I stood in line at security, waiting to go through the inspection point and board the Oceanic *Aphrodite.* For the first time, I'd be dancing the Talent Show finale at the end of the cruise, which needed to go flawlessly. My future depended on this event, so I practiced every possible second.

My toes tapped in time with my thoughts, probably making me look quite odd. Fortunately, I'd been sailing this cruise for months as part of the onboard entertainment. The officers working the line knew me, and they were used to watching me dance in line. Once I made it to the metal detectors, it should be smooth sailing. Pun intended.

Normally, staff boarded the ship the night before or early in the morning before any guests arrived. My cabin mate Penny and I had gotten special permission to spend the night off-ship, a privilege that likely wouldn't be repeated now that her guy problems made us two hours late. At least they'd agreed to let us on right after the VIPs so we could beat most of the regular passengers.

Beside me, Penny tapped away on her phone, her long dark hair forming a curtain over the device. "Why hasn't Robbie texted me back?"

"I'm sure you'll hear from him soon." I struggled to keep from revealing my true feelings on the subject. "Especially since he'll be on the ship. It's not like he can avoid you forever."

Her head shot up, brown eyes flashing. "You think he's avoiding me?"

In truth, yes, I did. But if I hadn't been distracted thinking about our upcoming performance, I would have found a nicer way to say so. Well, probably. I'd been trying to politely tell her what a creep Robbie was for weeks, and she hadn't listened. Maybe it was time to be more direct. "I think he enjoys the rich passengers who might further his career once he graduates. Rob's pretty clear on his priorities, and you're not one of them."

"Ouch." Her face twisted into a grimace. A pang hit me. "I hope you're wrong."

"So do I, Pen. So do I." Not knowing what else to say, I changed the subject. "I'm excited that Max is letting us do the finale this week."

"Oh, I know! It's going to be amazing! The guests won't know what hit 'em. Especially the stuffy old farts who think pole dancing is only for strippers."

Despite myself, I blanched.

A look of horror crossed her face. "Oh, no. I'm sorry, Janey."

She hadn't meant to insult me, but I'd learned pole while working strip clubs. The patrons loved blue-eyed blondes, so owners always wanted someone with my look.

"It's fine," I said, breaking the awkward silence.

If things went well this week, the two of us would be cemented as dancing partners for the next year of cruises or more. Each additional performance meant cash in our pockets. I could ignore one thoughtless comment in the interests of continuing to pay for my father's assisted living every month. Dad had nowhere else to go, especially since his disability left him unable to care for himself.

Needing to look at anything else, I turned to face the metal detectors separating us from the ship's boarding area. The line of people might as well be a wall. I shifted from one six-inch heel to the other, wondering what this week's hold-up was. Last week, a bride didn't understand why her father couldn't bring his actual guns to her "shotgun" wedding. The week before, a groom tried to bring a case of whiskey, which is against ship policy. Maybe we had a celebrity up ahead. They always slowed down security. Rumor had it that some famous baseball player was getting married onboard this week. I didn't follow sports, though, so unless he wore his uniform, I'd never know.

Craning my neck to see the inevitable shenanigans at the front of the line, I almost didn't hear the commotion behind me. A woman gasped, then a child cried out. I turned to see what was happening, a fraction of a second too late.

A man's voice yelled, "Look out!"

Seconds later, something shoved me from behind, hard. Stumbling, I wheeled my arms for balance. The heel cracked off my shoe. I tumbled to the ground, landing hard on my hip. Ouch. As a dancer, I'm no stranger to injuries, but that was going to leave a bruise. It stung, almost as much as the realization that I was going to have to replace my two hundred dollar Pleasers—and with no time to go shopping before we set sail, I'd have to do it at one of the ship's outrageously overpriced boutiques. Entertainment staff got a discount, but not nearly enough. Silently, I kissed this week's earnings good-bye. At least I didn't have to pay for my room, utilities, or food.

"Are you okay?" The same voice asked.

Blinking several times to clear the pain clouding my vision,

I looked up to see such a delicious-looking man bending over me, I wondered if I imagined him. Curly brown hair falling across his forehead, light brown eyes the color of a latte, high cheekbones, a strong nose, and perfect lips. This face belonged in a museum.

"Gorgeous," I said without thinking. Then I flushed. "I mean, yes. I'm okay. What happened?"

His lips twitched at my slip of the tongue. "Runaway baggage cart. You were nearly murdered by a wedding dress. What an unfortunate end for such a talented fidgeter."

"You saw me dancing?"

"I may have noticed you before the cart rolled away."

The admission made me smile. "Well, thanks. If you hadn't been here, I might have been flattened."

"Glad I could help." He held out a hand to pull me to my feet. Our eyes locked, and suddenly, I couldn't breathe. "I'm Frank."

"Janey. Nice to meet you." As perfected over the years, I kept my face and tone pleasant but not overly friendly. As hot as this guy was, passengers were strictly forbidden. I didn't want to spend the entire cruise wishing he wasn't. Dropping his hand, I moved away from him, back toward the line.

A wince of pain sent me looking for the nearest chair. The fall must've twisted my ankle, and I'd been too distracted by this man to notice. Frank had shifted away, following my lead, but now he returned to my side. "Are you okay?"

"It's nothing. I'll walk it off."

"Let me see."

"It's no big deal," I insisted. "I'm a dancer. Happens far more often than it should."

"That's unfortunate, but please let me see it. It's my fault you're hurt, and I'm a doctor."

"Don't worry about me. Penny, are you okay?"

My friend stood nearby, her face unreadable. "It missed me

by a mile. But I'm a little dizzy. I've got to go. I'll see you onboard."

Before I could tell her not to go call deadbeat Robbie again, she vanished in the direction of the women's restroom, one hand resting on her stomach. Poor thing. My friend needed me, and I wanted to go with her, but my throbbing ankle stopped me. I didn't want to spent more time falling under Dr. Frank's spell, but the line to get onto the ship—and to the infirmary—hadn't budged. Better to sit and let him check me out than stand in pain, balancing on a broken shoe.

Together, we hobbled to a bench near the entrance to the security line. It wasn't nearly as far away as it should have been after twenty minutes of waiting. I collapsed with a sigh. Then my eyes landed on something and I groaned. "Oh, no."

"What's wrong?" Frank asked.

"My carry-on is still in the line. I need to grab it before someone reports it to security as an unattended bag."

"Is it that green one?" He pointed at my battered duffel, now sitting a bit outside the line, probably pushed by an overeager passenger. "That's all you need for a week?"

The bag only contained a few things I'd taken to spend the night at my sister's apartment, playing dress-up with my five-year-old niece. Easily the best thing about having a home port in Miami. Everything else remained in the cabin Penny and I shared. This passenger didn't need to know that.

"Yeah."

"Don't move." He touched my shoulder as he walked away, sending an unexpected jolt of desire through me. Oh, no. The last thing I needed was to get involved with a passenger, and this one could be trouble.

As my savior walked away, I marveled at his straight back, the way he held his head erect. The man moved with confi-dence, but also an innate grace, like a cat. Or a dancer. He didn't walk, he glided across the floor. I also took in the lines of his windbreaker, the creases of his pants, the leather of the shoes molding to his feet perfectly. Dr. Frank was off-limits for more reasons than one. Rich men only ever wanted one thing from girls like me, and I wasn't in a position to give it.

A moment later, he returned, my bag slung over his shoulder. I thanked him, then lifted my injured leg to rest on top once he set it in front of me. The pain subsided, so I scooted down to rest my head on top of the bench. Perfect. Except for being late to work and the throbbing ankle.

"I'm going to check you out now, okay?"

It was on the tip of my tongue to mention that I'd been checking him out for the last five minutes, but flirting with passengers needed to remain subtler, more innocent. I nodded. His touch was firm, yet soft. He poked and prodded for a moment while I did my best not to wince.

Finally, he said, "It's not broken."

Relief washed over me. If I broke my ankle, I'd be out of a job. While I loved my sister and niece, I didn't want to move in with them after becoming unemployed and homeless. "Thank goodness."

"Wrap it up for a couple of days, try to stay off it, and you should be fine. The infirmary will have elastic bandages."

"I've got one in my bag, actually," I said, opening a zipper on the side. "Part of the job."

"Excellent! Please, allow me."

I should say no, do it myself. After all, I'd wrapped various body parts a thousand times. But the smallest innocent touch couldn't hurt anything. His firm hands warmed my ankle, making it feel better already. Once we got on the ship, I'd never see him again. "Thanks."

He took the bandage and expertly wrapped my ankle in a matter of seconds. His hand lingered, just enough for me to notice. This magnetic pull between us wasn't one-sided. "There you go."

For the first time, I noticed how close he stood. The heat of his breath washed over my cheek. My skin burned where he'd examined my ankle. I refused to let myself wonder what these fingers would feel like moving over the rest of my body. He licked his lips, and my eyes darted involuntarily to follow the movement. I became helpless to look away.

It had been a long time since I'd been with anyone. Too long. I made a mental note to find a suitable hookup at the first port. Suitable meaning not a passenger, and not while on the ship. Not if I wanted to keep my job, which I very much enjoyed.

"Are you part of the Sassy Singles?" I asked, naming a group that booked multiple activities for passengers interested in meeting someone.

"Me? No, I'm not looking for a relationship." Good. Neither was I. Not that it mattered. He continued. "But it cracks me up that they'd put a singles cruise on a ship called the *Aphrodite*."

"Well, legend has it that people fall in love on this ship. One day, and you'll meet your mate. Or so they say."

"Huh. Good thing I believe in science over myth then."

"Yeah," I said, shaking off an inexplicable twinge of disappointment. The legend was a marketing ploy; all the staff knew it. After all, we'd been sailing around for months without falling in love. But it sold tickets for the singles cruises.

"Francis!" A high-pitched voice broke the spell between us.

Over the doctor's shoulder I spotted a stunningly gorgeous woman in flawless heavy makeup, chestnut hair with the top half twisted elegantly into a sleek chignon, and a swingy white sundress with big pink flowers painted all over it.

"Over here," he called to the woman.

"Francis, huh?"

"It's a family name."

"I'm sure it is." The longer we talked, the more dangerously close I came to crossing a line, but I couldn't resist one more comment before reining it in. "After the first woman in the cabinet?"

He grinned. "How'd you guess?"

The question was a joke, so his response startled me. I blinked a couple of times to cover my surprise before responding. "My mother was a big *Dirty Dancing* fan. I've got that and *Lethal Weapon* memorized."

What I didn't mention was that those were the only two videos we'd owned. After Mom walked out on me and my sister, those movies were my only way of feeling connected to her. I wore out the DVDs, watching them over and over.

"A woman of refined tastes," he said.

Before I could respond, the woman arrived at Frank's side, placing a perfectly manicured hand on his shoulder. She said nothing, her expression stormy, eyes hidden behind sunglasses the size of Disney World.

"Hey, Lisa," he said. "Is it time?"

"'Is it time?'" she mimicked, her face twisting into a grimace. "Duh! We're going to be late! Get your butt in line."

Girlfriend? Wife? No. No rings on either of them. My heart sank. Of course a man like Frank would have a girlfriend. Charming, sexy, rich, a doctor who moved with the grace of a dancer? The fact that I'd spent even half a second thinking he might be available made me flush with embarrassment. Especially when he'd said he wasn't looking for a relationship—he wouldn't be if he were here with someone.

On the other hand, this *was* a singles cruise, so maybe there was hope. The two of them had similar coloring, the same nose. As I took in the shapes of their faces, I'd bet my favorite Pleasers that she was related to Frank.

With a sigh, I glanced at my feet. Second favorite pair, anyway. These were toast.

"We can't be late. The ship isn't going to disembark with

VIP passengers waiting to go through the security line," he said, but he stood to follow her.

Of course he was a VIP. The sunglasses pushed casually on top of his head cost more than half my Pleasers collection. The shoes I needed for work and had been accumulating slowly over the past ten years, most of them from eBay. We didn't move in the same circles. I couldn't even afford to window shop in his world.

"What if it does, though? Won't you feel terrible?" She spoke slowly, as if addressing an unintelligent child. She must be an older sister; younger siblings never got away with talking like that. I had to believe Frank wouldn't date someone who treated him like something stuck to the bottom of her shoe. "I can't believe this. I should be sipping champagne right now."

I craned my neck up to meet her eyes from my seated position. "The VIP passengers are the first to board. You'll have over an hour to relax and explore the ship while the non-VIPs are going through security downstairs. Unless you turn around and leave the port area, you'll be fine."

"Thanks," the woman said icily. She gave me a practiced once over before turning back to Frank. "Who is this and why are you talking to her instead of going through security?"

"I'm Janey. I work—"

She put her hand out in the 'stop' sign. "That's nice. We have to go."

"So, uh, that's my sister," Frank said as Lisa stalked away. Unlike her brother, she moved like a linebacker.

"Seems delightful."

"Being late stresses her out. She's usually not so bad. Anyway, looks like we made it to the front of the line." A couple watched us from the space directly in front of the metal detectors as Lisa walked through. Frank gestured at them. "Those are my friends, Jake and Margie. Do you want to join us so you don't have to wait?"

From the other side of security, Lisa turned, hands on hips. "Francis Hanson, now!"

If the rest of his party was anything like her, the last thing I wanted was to hang out with them. "Thanks, but I'll wait for Penny. I don't want to get on your sister's bad side."

"You're right about that." He laughed. "I've got to go. Sorry."

"It's cool. Thanks again for saving me." Before I finished my sentence, he'd jogged off to meet his party.

Watching him go, I sighed. Well, it was a nice moment, before Lisa showed up. Probably for the best, given our circumstances.

I pulled myself upright, testing my sore ankle. Not terrible, not great. I was supposed to dance in this evening's welcome show, though, and that might not be possible.

Digging around in my bag, I found a pair of flip flops in the bottom. Switching shoes helped. Then I went to find Penny. She hadn't gone far, standing outside the bathroom near the row of pay phones. In all my months working for the cruise line, this was the first time I'd seen anyone looking like they might use one.

I didn't ask if she'd managed to get through to Robbie, preferring to believe she hadn't tried. I was afraid she used a pay phone to try to trick him into answering her call, which made me sad. Penny deserved so much better. At least she put her phone away and returned to the line with me.

The rest of the VIPs had finished going through security and waited for the gangway to open. Through the crowd, I spotted the captain's hat bobbing toward the giant glass doors. A glance at the clock on the wall told me he would be boarding soon, and this area would clear out quickly.

Scooping up my bag, I went through the line in record time. The throbbing in my ankle had dulled to an ache, and I thought about finding Dr. Frank to thank him again. Probably a bad idea, given the chemistry between us, but also the polite thing to do.

Then I spotted him, through the glass separating the waiting area from the docks. He walked about five steps behind the Captain. Beside him strode Lisa, the couple from the security line, and two people I recognized with a start. Only very special guests got priority boarding, which reinforced that this guy was way out of my league. But what sealed our lack of fate was the person who walked beside Frank's friend: my boss, Max Weiss.

Consorting with the passengers was strictly prohibited. If I did anything beyond extremely innocent flirtation with Frank, and Max found out about it, I would get fired and left at the nearest port.

Ahead of Max walked the ship owner's very beautiful, very single daughter, Nellie. In response to something Frank said, she threw her head back, letting out a laugh I knew from experience was throaty and very sexy. Where Nellie went, heads turned. I couldn't begin to compete with her, even if doing so wouldn't cost me my job. As I watched, she reached out and touched Frank on the shoulder. He slung one arm around her casually in an intimate gesture. My heart sank.

Time for this particular fantasy to sail off into the horizon.

Want to read on? Visit www.lauraheffernan.com and sign up for my newsletter to get it delivered within minutes.

# About the Author

Laura Heffernan writes fun, witty romantic comedies and more serious women's fiction. After a few years of practicing law, she realized that she much preferred arguing with her characters rather than other people. It's easier to win that way.

When not watching total strangers get married, drag racing queens, or cooking competitions, Laura enjoys board games, travel, board games, baking, and board games. She lives in the northeast with her husband, the world's most active toddler, and two furry little beasts.

Laura loves connecting with readers. Find her on **Facebook** or on **Twitter**, where she spends far too much time tweeting about reality TV and Canadian chocolate. Sign up for news and updates at **http://www.lauraheffernan.com/**.

## The Reality Star Series

*America's Next Reality Star:* Jen went on a reality show to compete for the $250,000 grand prize. But when she finds herself battling another woman for co-competitor Justin's love, she finds herself wondering what the true prize is.

*Sweet Reality:* After a killer competitor threatens her new business, Jen sets sail on a new reality show adventure to save the day. But Ariana's back, and she's determined to end Jen and Justin's relationship once and for all.

*Reality Wedding:* After retiring from reality TV, Jen receives an offer she can't refuse. The Network wants Jen and Justin to film their wedding to fill an empty time slot—and if they refuse, the Network will get Justin fired.

## The Gamer Girls Series

*She's Got Game*: Gwen's dedicated to becoming the American Board Games Champion, and she never ever mixes gaming with pleasure. But when she meets Cody, trying to resist his charm becomes a losing proposition.

*Against the Rules*: For years, Holly has harbored a secret crush on her best friend's dad. Nathan is young, he's hot. What's a little harmless flirtation while playing games? But when she discovers that Nathan returns her feelings, Holly may have to choose between two of the most important people in her life.

*Make Your Move*: Shannon's more interested in designing games and rising to the top at work than dating. She's surprised to find herself falling for her roommate, Tyler. Worse, he's dating her boss's daughter. If she makes her move, Tyler's girlfriend could get Shannon fired.

❧

## Push and Pole Series

*Poll Dancer:* A delightfully modern twist on *My Fair Lady*: When a promotional video for her pole-dancing classes goes viral, Mel comes under fire from a local politician running for senate. Desperate to save her studio, Mel decides her only option is to launch her own campaign — and win!

*The Accidental Senator*: After accidentally finding herself elected state senator, Lana Chen is determined to prove her worth. But when a mistake aids the passage of a bill that's going to put her best friend out of business, Lana has to find a way to set things right before it's too late.

❧

## Retail to Riches Series

*A Royal Farce:* After years of secretly crushing on her friend Pierre, Lila is thrilled when he proposes they start a fake relationship. For weeks, she finds herself hoping their farce could turn into the real thing—but Pierre's hiding a secret of royal magnitude.

A Royal Pain: **Coming Soon**

❧

## Standalone Books

*Finding Tranquility:* Jess Cooper lost her husband on 9/11. Just not the way she thought. On September 11, 2001, Brett enters Logan Airport bearing a ticket for a flight that crashes into the World Trade Center. Jess knows her husband is gone. She doesn't know he never boarded that plane. Years later, Jess is shocked to meet Christa and recognize her spouse. She's more shocked to realize their love may have survived.

*Anna's Guide to Getting Even:* Anna's perfect life has turned into a string of disasters: After a hurricane destroys her house, her ex publicizes private photos of her — which costs Anna her job and her current boyfriend. And after hitting rock bottom, she decides that revenge is the only way forward…

*Friction:* Britt's always avoided relationships. Then, weeks before she's set to move away, she meets Colin. To her surprise, she finds herself wanting more.

*Time of My Life:* She's a poor dance teacher. He's her rich student. If they can only overcome their differences, this could be love. A gender-flipped update of *Dirty Dancing.*

**Welcome to Shady Grove...**

**Aly doesn't believe in psychics. Too bad she just had a vision.**

Future scientists don't have visions. Aly's got enough on her plate, with finishing her degree and taking care of her nephew and starting her new job at the antique store while drooling over the owner's gorgeous son. No visions.

Alas, the universe doesn't care what Aly believes. When she turns 21, she starts to feel psychic impressions left on objects. A disorienting power for someone surrounded by antiques. Then cranky customer Earl is killed, and Aly's new boss Olive is the prime suspect. Who hated Earl enough to kill? Police would rather make a quick arrest than investigate, so it's up to Aly to clear Olive's name.

Shady Grove is reeling from the first murder in decades. If Aly can get her hands on the murder weapon, she should be able to solve the crime. Can she learn to control her visions before the killer sets their sights on her?

*Mystic Pieces*
*The Scry's the Limit*
*Sight Seering*
*Mystic Treasure*
*Seer Today, Gone Tomorrow*